TRESPASSERS

BY BREENA BARD

AN IMPRINT OF

SCHOLASTIC

FOR MOM, DAD, MEAGAN, AND SHAWN, AND ALL OF OUR LAKE ADVENTURES

Library of Congress Control Number: 2019909123

ISBN 978-1-338-26423-4 (hardcover)
ISBN 978-1-338-26421-0 (paperback)

10 9 8 7 6 5 4 3 2 1   20 21 22 23 24

Printed in China 38
First edition, May 2020
Author photo by Weeno Photography
Edited by Adam Rau & David Saylor
Book design by Phil Falco
Publisher: David Saylor

Flip
Flip
SAND
LAKE
30 miles
SNAP!

Flip
Flip
Flip

FLIP
SNAP!

Flip

MURDER ON THE ORIENT EXPRESS
AGATHA CHRISTIE
Flip

Flip
SNAP!

Flip

Flip

SNAP!
I WIN!

ARE WE THERE YET?
ANOTHER HALF HOUR, GABBY.

PLAY AGAIN?
NAH, I'M OVER SNAP.

HEY, GABBY, WANNA PLAY CHEAT?

I'M READING.

YOU'RE *ALWAYS* READING.

SO? YOU CAN PLAY WITH MORGAN.
Flip

IT'S NO FUN WITH JUST TWO PLAYERS!

LEAVE HER ALONE, SIMON.
LET'S JUST PLAY WAR.

AW MAN...
WAR IS SO BORING!

ALL RIGHT, ONE LAST STOP BEFORE THE LAKE.
EVERYONE SAY HI TO PAUL!
Paul Bunyan's
-SUPERMARKET-
HI, PAUL!

WATERMELON
.50/lb

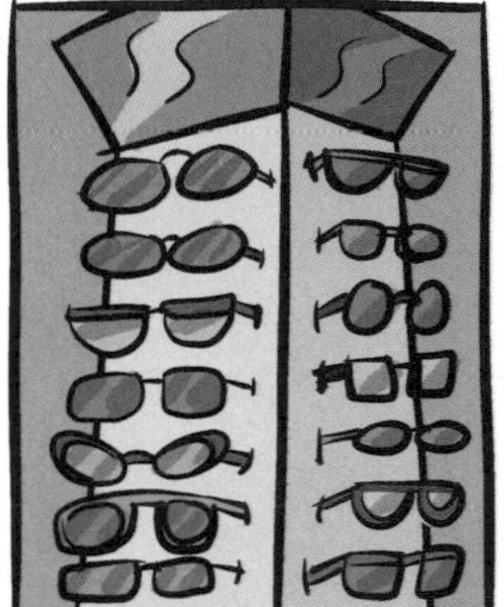

SMORES!
MALLOWS
MALLOWS
MALLOWS
CHOCOLATE
CHOCOLATE
CHOCOLATE
CHOCOLATE
CHOCOLATE
CHOCOLATE
GRAHAM
GRAHAM
GRAHAM

OKAY, EVERYONE PICK OUT A FEW THINGS YOU'D LIKE.
SWOOSH
It's the SUMMER SODA!
INFO
ICE

AND LET'S PICK OUT A FEW ***HEALTHY*** FOODS TOO, OKAY?
YEAH! ***SUGAR POPPERS!***
COOL CORN
COOL CORN
PUFFY RICE
SUGAR POPPERS
BRAN BARN
BRAN BARN
WHEAT WHAT
FLAKE FUN
FLAKE FUN

DUMP
SUGAR POPPERS

CEREAL
I'M GONNA CHECK OUT THE MAGAZINES.
ME TOO!
4
3

MAGAZINES
ROMANCE
BAIT & TACKLE
MYSTERY
SCI-FI
GLAM
POP!
TECH TIME

THE MALTESE FALCON

AGATHA CHRISTIE
AND THEN THERE WERE NONE

THE WESTING GAME

GLAM
GLAM!
MURDER ON THE NILE

GABBY, YOU CAN'T POSSIBLY READ ALL THOSE IN ONE WEEK.

YEAH, I CAN!

OKAY, I KNOW ***TECHNICALLY*** YOU CAN...

BUT MAYBE YOU SHOULD SPEND A LITTLE TIME JUST HAVING FUN.
MAGAZINES & BOOKS
BEST SELLERS
WHO SAYS A STACK OF BOOKS ISN'T FUN?
STEP
STEP

I KNOW...
YEAH, I KNOW THAT.

BAIT & TACKLE
WHO'S DAD TALKING TO?
PROBABLY WORK.
THIS IS TERRIBLE TIMING.

YOU KNOW WE LEAVE FOR VACATION TODAY!

AGAZINES BOOKS
BEST SELLERS
LOOK, GREG, I CAN'T TALK RIGHT NOW. I'LL CALL YOU LATER.
BAIT & TACKLE
MAPS
LIVE BAIT

WHAT'S UP, DAD?
HEY, GABBY.

JUST GETTING US OUR FISHING LICENSES.
MOM IS EXPECTING US TO CATCH DINNER TOMORROW!
YUCK!

HOW ABOUT YOU PICK OUT SOME NIGHT CRAWLERS?
SURE.
JUICY ONES!
MAPS
LIVE BAIT

IS EVERYTHING OKAY?
YEAH...

I WISH THEY'D GIVE ME A STRAIGHT ANSWER.
SIGH.

10
11
12
13
HEY DAD!

CAN WE GET SOME FIREWORKS?
FIREWORKS
TNT

BUT WE ALREADY HAVE NATURE'S FIREWORKS...
FIREFLIES!
pleeeease? MOM?
FIREWORKS
OH YES, WE *HAVE* TO GET FIREWORKS...

WE ALWAYS SET SOME OFF HERE WHEN WE WERE KIDS!

OKAY, BUT NO ***UNSUPERVISED*** PYROTECHNICS. WE'LL LIGHT THEM OFF TOGETHER.
15
CHECKOUT
1
2
3
YES!

GEEZ, GABBY, MORE BOOKS?
SO?

DID YOU EVEN PICK OUT ***ANY*** SNACKS?
TNT

I THINK IT'S GREAT THAT GABBY LOVES TO READ.

BESIDES, SIMON...
1
YOU GRABBED ENOUGH SNACKS FOR THE WHOLE LAKE!
BOOP
BOOP
FIREWORKS

OKAY, KIDS, ALL OF YOU GET IN FRONT OF PAUL BUNYAN FOR A PICTURE.
ICE

HONEY, YOU SHOULD GET IN THERE TOO.

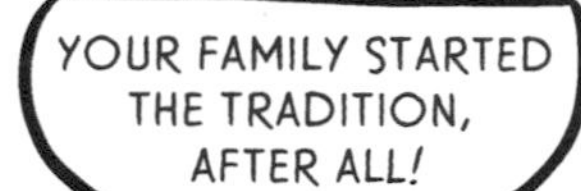
YOUR FAMILY STARTED THE TRADITION, AFTER ALL!

WHY DON'T YOU ALL GET INTO THE PHOTO?

I ***THINK*** I KNOW HOW TO WORK ONE OF THOSE FANCY PHONE CAMERAS.
SHERIFF RIVERA!
PAUL BUNYAN

ALL RIGHT, EVERYBODY SAY, "CHEESE!"
I THINK THAT'S A KEEPER.
THANKS!
GOLLY, I CAN'T BELIEVE HOW BIG YOU KIDS HAVE GROWN!

ANY NEWS IN TOWN THIS SUMMER?
IT'S BEEN PRETTY QUIET THIS SUMMER.

LIKE EVERYONE, WE'VE ALL BEEN MOSTLY TRANSFIXED BY THE BIG LUMENS TRIAL DOWN IN CHICAGO.

YEAH, WE HEARD HE GOT A LUCKY BREAK.

HE'S GOT GOOD LAWYERS, THAT'S WHAT.

WON'T FIND MUCH OF THAT DRAMA UP HERE!

THANK GOODNESS. WE'RE LOOKING FORWARD TO A RELAXING WEEK!

HERE WE ARE, HOME AWAY FROM HOME!
HENDERSON
WOODS
JACOBSON

THERE'S GENE!

LOOK AT HIM SWING THAT AX.
CHOP

NOW REMEMBER, GUYS, IT WAS ONLY THIS PAST DECEMBER THAT HE LOST EMMY...

HE'S PROBABLY STILL GRIEVING, AND HE MIGHT NOT BE HIS USUAL JOVIAL SELF.

YEAH, MAYBE GIVE HIM A LITTLE SPACE THIS WEEK. BE FRIENDLY BUT NOT OBNOXIOUS, OKAY?

OKAY.
OF COURSE.
GENE!

WELL, HELLO THERE, NEIGHBORS!
HEY, GENE! WE MISSED YOU!

I WAS STARTING TO THINK I WOULDN'T GET TO SEE YOU FOLKS AT ALL THIS SUMMER!
TRUST ME, WE WOULD HAVE LOVED TO COME UP HERE EARLIER.

HOW ABOUT YOU, GENE? HOW ARE YOU HOLDING UP?

I'M NOT GONNA LIE, IT'S BEEN REAL LONELY HERE WITHOUT EMMY.
BUT BOY AM I GLAD TO HAVE YOU FOLKS NEXT DOOR AGAIN!

YOU DON'T NEED YOUR SPACE?
SIMON!
MY SPACE? GOODNESS NO!
I'VE HAD ENOUGH SPACE ALL WINTER AND SPRING.

WHAT I NEED IS SOME QUALITY TIME WITH THE WOODS FAMILY.

HEY, I THOUGHT THE JACOBSONS WERE SELLING THEIR PLACE?
THEY DID! THOSE ARE THE NEW NEIGHBORS, THE MARTINS.
A COUPLE FROM CHICAGO AND THEIR TWO KIDS. THEY'VE BEEN HERE A FEW WEEKS NOW.

I HAVEN'T SEEN THEM ON THE LAKE MUCH, BUT I STOPPED BY AND SAID HELLO.

WE'LL HAVE TO GO INTRODUCE OURSELVES.

PAUL BUNYAN'S

CHESS
LIFE
MONOPOLY
Scattergories
CLUE
OPERATION
Trivial Pursuit
Kitten Puzzle

JUST HOW WE WE LEFT IT, HUH, GABBY?
PLUS A FEW SPIDERS, YEAH.
PAUL BUNYANS
PAUL BUNYANS

DIBS ON THE TOP BUNK!
GABBY, YOU'RE THE ONLY ONE WHO WANTS THE TOP BUNK.

LATER

READY TO MAKE SOME WAVES?
I'M GONNA BRING MY BOOK ALONG!

I THINK WE'LL BE TOO BUSY EXPLORING FOR YOU TO READ MUCH!

IF WE'RE NOT BACK BY DINNER, SEND OUT A SEARCH PARTY!

AND AWAY WE GO!

LOOK, GABBY, IT'S YOUR FAVORITE PLACE ON THE LAKE!

HAVE YOU EVER SEEN ANYONE UP THERE?

I HAVEN'T SEEN A SOUL FOR AS LONG AS WE'VE BEEN COMING TO THE LAKE.

IT'S PROBABLY WORTH A FORTUNE.

DID *ANYONE* EVER LIVE THERE?
OH, I'M SURE AT SOME POINT.

YOU'LL HAVE TO ASK YOUR MOM ABOUT THAT.

SHE WOULD HAVE BEEN HERE ABOUT THE TIME IT WAS BUILT.
SHE WAS PROBABLY AROUND YOUR AGE, GABBY.

IT'S KIND OF **CREEPY.**

I AGREE. NOW, WHO'S HUNGRY?

Shhhuck!

Ssslice

Sizzle

SO WHILE YOU GUYS WERE OUT ON THE LAKE, MOM AND I MET THE NEW NEIGHBORS.
OH YEAH?

JUST THE HUSBAND AND WIFE. THEY STOPPED BY TO SAY HELLO.

THEY WERE KIND OF...

WEIRD.

OH, MORGAN, I WOULDN'T SAY "WEIRD."
THEY WERE ***TOTALLY*** WEIRD!

THE LADY WAS OVERLY FRIENDLY, LIKE SHE WAS ***HIDING*** SOMETHING.

AND HER HUSBAND WOULDN'T MAKE EYE CONTACT AT ALL!

THEY *WERE* A LITTLE UNUSUAL.

THAT'S JUST A NICE WAY TO SAY "WEIRD."

MAYBE THEY'RE CRIMINALS ON THE LAM!

HEY, IT'S NOT CRAZY. JOHN DILLINGER... AL CAPONE...
LOTS OF CRIMINALS HIDE OUT IN THE NORTH WOODS!

THAT'S WHAT WE'RE DOING HERE, ISN'T IT?
HA-HA.

DID YOU MEET THE TWO KIDS?

NO, WE DIDN'T SEE THEM.
THEY'RE ABOUT YOUR AGE THOUGH. I'M SURE YOU'LL MEET THEM.

OKAY, FOURTH WORD...
WATCH!
TIME!

TIME MOVING...
FORWARD...
FUTURE!

OH! BACK TO THE FUTURE!
SNAP

THAT'S IT!

YEAH!
SLAP
WOO-HOO!

THAT WAS TOO EASY.

OKAY, COME ON, GAB. BOOK DOWN, LET'S SHOW 'EM HOW IT'S *REALLY* DONE.

Set

unfold

Grab

Dial "M" for Murder

OKAY, MOVIE.

FOUR WORDS.

KNOCK KNOCK

HANG ON. I'LL SEE WHO IT IS.

OH, HI THERE!
OH, I SEE. SOUNDS FUN.

JUST A MINUTE, I'LL GO GET THEM.

GABBY, SIMON, IT'S THE KIDS FROM NEXT DOOR. THEY CAME TO SEE IF YOU WANT TO HANG OUT.

WE'RE PLAYING A GAME!

WE CAN FINISH WHEN YOU GET BACK.

BUT WE DON'T EVEN *KNOW* THEM!

THIS IS HOW YOU *GET* TO KNOW THEM!

YEAH, WHO KNOWS...
THEY COULD BE YOUR NEW BEST BUDS!

HI.
HEY.

UH, OUR DAD SAID YOU WANTED TO HANG OUT WITH US?

OUR MOM *MADE* US COME OVER HERE.
CHICAGO

I'M PAIGE AND THIS IS BRYAN.
POKE
POKE
CHICAGO
BEARS

GRAB

HEY!
SNAP

WELL, I'M GABBY AND THIS IS MY BROTHER, SIMON.

WHAT GRADE ARE YOU GUYS IN?
I'M STARTING 6TH AND PAIGE IS IN 8TH.
COOL, SAME AS US!

SO, DO YOU GUYS LIVE UP HERE OR SOMETHING? LIKE, ARE YOU "COUNTRY FOLK"?
HA-HA!
CHICAGO BEARS

YEAH, DO YOU, LIKE, PLAY THE BANJO?
CHICAGO BEARS

WHAT? NO, WE'RE ON VACATION. WE LIVE IN GREEN BAY. THE CITY.

WHY, WHERE ARE YOU GUYS FROM?
CHICAGO. I ***WISH*** WE WERE STILL THERE.
ME TOO.

IT'S ACTUALLY REALLY NICE UP HERE.
YEAH, YOU GUYS MIGHT LIKE IT.

WE DON'T EVEN GET CELL PHONE SERVICE OUT HERE.
CHICAGO BEARS

WHAT DO YOU GUYS EVEN *DO* HERE?
FLICK

THERE'S TONS OF STUFF TO DO!

SWIMMING, KAYAKING...
FISHING, MINI GOLF...
HORSE SHOES...

RIGHT, GABBY?

I LIKE TO JUST SIT BY THE WATER AND READ!
OKAY, NEVER MIND, DON'T ASK HER.
CHICAGO BEARS

YEAH GROSS. LET'S JUST GO FOR A WALK OR SOMETHING.
CHICAGO BEARS

I LIKE YOUR SWEATSHIRT. WE'RE PACKERS FANS THOUGH, RIGHT, SIMON?
UH-HUH.
I DON'T CARE ABOUT FOOTBALL. I JUST WEAR THIS 'CUZ IT'S GOOD FOR CERTAIN... "EXTRACURRICULAR" ACTIVITIES.

YOU KNOW WHAT I MEAN?
SHE *MEANS* SHOPLIFTING.
FLICK

Reach

M-80

GIVE ME YOUR LIGHTER, BRYAN.

GIMME A FIRECRACKER, THEN.
NO WAY, GET YOUR OWN!

SHE STEALS THEM FROM OUR UNCLE.
FLICK

GIVE ME YOUR LIGHTER, YOU TURD!
HEY!

YOU **STUPID JERK,** GIVE THAT BACK!

UM...
WHAT ARE YOU DOING?
IS THAT AN M-80?

YOU CAN'T LIGHT THAT! THOSE ARE *ILLEGAL!*

OH NO, ARE YOU SOME KIND OF JUNIOR POLICE OFFICER?

NO, IT'S JUST...

THOSE THINGS ARE DANGEROUS! YOU COULD BLOW OFF YOUR FINGER.
OKAY GEEZ.
DON'T GET SO BENT OUT OF SHAPE!
WHERE ARE WE GOING, ANYWAY?

WE'RE JUST TAKING A WALK.
WHAT'S THE POINT OF THAT?
CHICAGO
BEARS

GOOD QUESTION. WHY *ARE* WE DOING THIS?
IT WAS YOUR IDEA!
BEARS

WELL, ***THIS*** IS REALLY EXCITING.
BEARS

ONE TIME WE WERE TAKING A WALK OUT HERE AND GABBY GOT FIRE ANTS IN HER PANTS!

SHE HAD TO WALK HOME WITH NO PANTS ON!
HA! THAT'S HILARIOUS!
IT WASN'T HILARIOUS, IT WAS PAINFUL!

FIRE ANTS ARE THE COOLEST.
I BEG TO DIFFER.

WHOA, GUYS, SHUT UP!
WHAT IS THIS PLACE?

HAVE WE WANDERED INTO BEVERLY HILLS?

THIS PLACE IS *KILLER!*

WHY DIDN'T MOM AND DAD BUY THIS PLACE?
SERIOUSLY.
SIMON, I THINK THIS IS THAT PLACE ON THE BLUFF!

WHO LIVES HERE? ANYONE FAMOUS?
CHICAGO

NOBODY LIVES HERE. NOT NOW, ANYWAY.

THEN LET'S GO CHECK IT OUT!

BRYAN, GET DOWN! WE CAN'T GO IN THERE!
BEARS

WHY NOT?

'CUZ IT'S TRESPASSING!

YEAH, IT'S CALLED "LIVE A LITTLE."

NO, WE CAN'T.

ALL RIGHT, WHATEVER.

FORGET IT. WE'RE GOING HOME, THEN.
LAME!

MILK
MILK
POPPER

RHINELANDER
WISCONSIN

GOOD MORNING, EVERYONE!
GOOD MORNING!
LOOKS LIKE A *BEAUTIFUL* DAY FOR SOME FISHING!

HEY, WHY DON'T WE INVITE THE NEW NEIGHBORS ALONG?

NO!
I MEAN, UM...

CAN'T THIS JUST BE A FAMILY THING?

LET'S TRY A FEW CASTS OVER HERE. I'VE GOT A GOOD FEELING.

GABBY, MORGAN, YOU NEED ANY HELP GETTING A WORM ON YOUR HOOK?
HM? OH, SURE.

ICK, I CAN'T SUPPORT THIS ANIMAL CRUELTY.
I'M USING A RUBBER WORM!

NO BITES YET?

OOH, I GOT ONE!
I THINK IT'S A BIG ONE!

Reel
Reel
Reel

SPLOOSH!

HA HA HA HA

HEY, MOM, WHAT'S THE DEAL WITH THE PLACE UP ON THE BLUFF?
IT'S SO FANCY, BUT IT ALWAYS LOOKS ABANDONED.

OH, THAT PLACE IS INTERESTING.

I WAS A LITLE GIRL WHEN THEY BUILT IT.

THE HOUSE WAS INCREDIBLY MODERN FOR ITS TIME. AN ARCHITECT FROM CHICAGO DESIGNED IT FOR HIS FASHION MODEL WIFE.
WOW! WHO WERE THEY?
THEIR NAMES WERE WALTER AND ANGELA GOLDSWORTH. IT WAS THEIR DREAM HOME.

IT PUT OUR LITTLE COTTAGE TO SHAME, BUT WE WERE PROUD TO LIVE NEAR SUCH A GLAMOROUS PLACE!

WERE YOU EVER INSIDE?
ONLY ONCE.

I WAS ABOUT YOUR AGE.

WALTER GOLDSWORTH WAS A VERY PRIVATE PERSON, BUT ONE NIGHT OUT OF THE BLUE HE THREW A BIG PARTY AND INVITED EVERYONE ON THE LAKE. WE WERE EXCITED TO GO. OF COURSE THEY ALSO INVITED A LOT OF THEIR FRIENDS FROM CHICAGO -- PEOPLE WITH MONEY AND IMPRESSIVE CAREERS.

I'D SEEN HIS WIFE, ANGELA, IN THE NEWSPAPER BEFORE, BUT IN PERSON SHE LOOKED EVEN MORE STUNNING.

LATER I LEARNED THAT THERE WAS SOMETHING GOING ON WITH THEM, BUT I HAD NO IDEA AT THE TIME.

I WAS JUST EXCITED MY PARENTS WERE LETTING ME STAY OUT SO LATE!

SHORTLY AFTER THAT PARTY, THE GOLDSWORTHS DISAPPEARED.

NO ONE SAW THEM LEAVE, THERE WERE NO MOVERS, NO MOVING VAN, NOTHING.
THEY JUST *VANISHED!*

GUESS YOU COULD SAY THIS LAKE HAS ITS VERY OWN MYSTERY.

I BET SOMEONE GOT ***MURDERED*** IN THERE!
NOW ***THAT*** SOUNDS LIKE A STORY!

YOU SHOULD WRITE IT, GABBY.
I'D LOVE TO READ YOUR VERSION OF WHAT HAPPENED WITHIN THOSE WALLS.

IN FACT, I MIGHT HAVE SOMETHING TO SPARK YOUR IMAGINATION...

I KNOW I USED TO KEEP IT BY THE PHOTO ALBUMS...

AH, HERE IT IS!

FLIP!
SAND LAKE REVIEW

I DON'T KNOW WHY I KEPT THIS PAPER ALL THESE YEARS...

I GUESS I JUST LIKED THIS PHOTO OF THEM.

"NEW IN TOWN"
Chicago Architect

BUT NOW IT MIGHT GET PUT TO CREATIVE USE!

LATER

Detective Longley took
a deep breath and

...WALKED THROUGH THE IRON GATES OF THE IMPRESSIVE LAKE HOUSE. HE HAD ATTENDED THE FANCY PARTY JUST TWO NIGHTS BEFORE, BUT TODAY'S VISIT WAS FOR A VERY DIFFERENT REASON.

NO ONE THOUGHT IT STRANGE THAT WALTER GOLDSWORTH HAD ONCE AGAIN RETREATED FROM THE PUBLIC EYE.

HIS WIFE, ANGELA, THE GLAMOROUS SUPERMODEL, WAS MORE SOCIAL. SO IT WAS HER DISAPPEARANCE THAT BEGAN TO RAISE QUESTIONS.

NOTHING OUT OF THE ORDINARY HAD HAPPENED AT THE PARTY.

THERE WAS NO FIGHTING OR TENSION BETWEEN THE HOSTS. THEN AGAIN, THOSE FANCY TYPES ALWAYS KEPT UP APPEARANCES, WHETHER THINGS WERE GOOD OR BAD.

BUT DETECTIVE LONGLEY KNEW WHEN SOMETHING WARRANTED A CLOSER LOOK.

SPEAKING OF A WARRANT, HE SHOULD PROBABLY GET ONE OF THOSE.
Tap
Tap

HE HAD A HUNCH THAT SOMETHING WASN'T RIGHT.

HEY.
AHH!

YOU *SCARED* ME!
SORRY. WHAT ARE YOU DOING?
UM, WRITING.
OH, IS IT FOR SCHOOL OR SOMETHING?
I HATE WHEN THEY GIVE HOMEWORK OVER VACATION.
NO, IT'S ACTUALLY...
IT'S JUST FOR FUN.
OH.
CAN I READ IT?
NO.
COME ON, LET ME READ IT. I CAN TELL YOU HOW BAD IT IS.
OH, REALLY NICE, PAIGE. LIKE I'M GONNA LET YOU READ IT NOW.
I'M JUST KIDDING, GEEZ! YOU'RE WAY TOO SERIOUS.
HUMPH.

I'M KIDDING! SO WHAT'S THIS MYSTERY ABOUT? WHO STOLE THE RUBBER FLOATIES? THE GREAT S'MORES CAPER?

HEY, GABBY! I HAVE TO SHOW YOU SOMETHING!

I'M KIND OF BUSY, SIMON.
WHAT IS IT, SOME DUMB SPIDER OR SOMETHING?

NO, COME ON, YOU'LL WANT TO SEE THIS!

IT'S IN THE OLD GARAGE.
HOW'D YOU GET IN THERE? IT'S ALWAYS LOCKED.

I HAVE MY WAYS.

OKAY, IT'S RIGHT OVER HERE.
I SWEAR, SIMON, IF IT'S A DEAD RAT OR SOMETHING...

IT'S NOT.
THIS SIDE UP

IT'S A CAT!

OH! IS IT HURT?
I DON'T THINK SO.

LOOK HOW FAT IT IS.
CAREFUL, IT MIGHT BITE!

NAH, IT'S A NICE, FAT KITTY!
PURR PURR
SEE?

ACTUALLY, I THINK SHE MIGHT BE PREGNANT.
REALLY?

I THINK SO. IF YOU TOUCH HER TUMMY THERE'S SOMETHING MOVING.
FEEL THAT?
YEAH, WEIRD.
WHAT SHOULD WE DO? SHOULD WE TAKE HER TO A VET?
MAYBE. LET'S LEAVE HER ALONE FOR NOW.
BYE FOR NOW, KITTY.
WHAT WERE YOU DOING IN HERE, ANYWAY?
EXPLORING!
I FOUND SOMETHING ELSE TOO.
GROSS! THOSE LOOK LIKE THEY'RE A HUNDRED YEARS OLD!
CIGARS
THE BOX IS PRETTY COOL THOUGH.
I'M GONNA LIGHT ONE!
YOU BETTER NOT!

LET'S NAME THE CAT SANDBOX, AFTER SAND LAKE.
CATS ALWAYS POOP IN SANDBOXES, GABBY.
HA-HA, GOOD POINT.

...GETTING SICK AND TIRED OF YOUR ATTITUDE, YOUNG LADY...

WELL I'M SICK OF ***YOUR*** STUPID ATTITUDE.
PAIGE MARTIN, YOU WATCH YOUR MOUTH!

NOW, I'LL ASK YOU ONE MORE TIME -- HOW MUCH DID YOU TAKE?

NO MORE THAN A JUDGE WOULD AWARD ME FOR YOUR CRAPPY PARENTING.

AGH! PAUL, COULD I GET A LITTLE HELP HERE? SHE'S YOUR DAUGHTER TOO!

LISTEN TO YOUR MOTHER.
YEAH RIGHT.
PAUL!

LOOK HERE, LITTLE MISS. YOU WILL PAY YOUR MOTHER BACK FOR WHATEVER YOU TOOK.
AND YOU'LL APOLOGIZE!
HUMPH.

THERE WILL BE CONSEQUENCES FOR YOUR BEHAVIOR.

THAT'S A JOKE COMING FROM YOU HYPOCRITES.

WHAT DID YOU JUST SAY?

THAT'S IT, I'M DONE PLAYING THIS GAME. YOU GET ONE MORE STRIKE, PAIGE!

THIS IS YOUR FINAL WARNING.
YEAH? AND THEN WHAT?

YOUNG LADY, YOU KNOW *EXACTLY* WHAT WILL HAPPEN THEN.
AND IT WON'T BE PRETTY.

TOOTH

SWIM

MORGAN, I THINK THE NEIGHBORS REALLY MIGHT BE CRIMINALS.
Spit

WHY DO YOU SAY THAT?

I OVERHEARD THEM TALKING, AND IT SOUNDED LIKE THEY WERE THREATENING THEIR DAUGHTER.

YOU SHOULDN'T EAVESDROP ON PEOPLE, GABBY.

I WASN'T!
YOU ALREADY HAVE A HYPERACTIVE IMAGINATION AS IT IS.
TELL THE KIDS?

OH ALSO, SIMON AND I SAW A PREGNANT CAT!
...DON'T KNOW, HONEY...
SWIM
WAIT, SHH!

OH, LOOK WHO'S EAVESDROPPING NOW!
SHH!

...DON'T NEED TO TELL THEM ANYTHING JUST YET. NOTHING IS CERTAIN UNTIL I TALK TO GREG TOMORROW.
NO REASON TO LET IT SPOIL OUR VACATION.
I GUESS WE KNEW THIS WAS COMING.

WHAT ARE THEY TALKING ABOUT?
...JUST BAD TIMING...

COME ON, LET'S GO TO BED.

WHAT WERE THEY TALKING ABOUT, MORGAN?
I DON'T KNOW, GABBY. LET'S JUST DROP IT, OKAY?

DID YOU SAY YOU SAW A PREGNANT CAT?

YEAH.

YOU'LL HAVE TO SHOW IT TO ME.

NIGHT, MORGAN.
GOOD-NIGHT.

NOTES

HAPPY WRITING, GABBY!
THANKS.

ANGELA'S BODY...
IN THE WARM GLOW OF THE MORNING SUN IT LOOKED ALMOST PEACEFUL, AS IF SHE WERE SLEEPING.
BUT SHE WAS CERTAINLY NOT.

WHEN WALTER FOUND HER LYING THERE HE WAS BESIDE HIMSELF.

HIS HEART RACED AS HE TRIED TO REMEMBER WHAT HAD OCCURRED THE NIGHT BEFORE.

HE VAGUELY RECALLED A HEATED DEBATE. OR WAS IT A FULL-BLOWN ARGUMENT?

HIS DREAD GREW WITH EVERY PASSING MINUTE. WALTER BEGAN TO WONDER IF, PERHAPS, HE HAD TAKEN HIS WIFE'S LIFE.
BUT I WOULD NEVER...

HE LOOKED DOWN AT HIS ACHING HANDS AND WAS TERRIFIED TO THINK WHAT HE MIGHT HAVE DONE WITH THEM.

THERE WERE TOO MANY UNANSWERABLE QUESTIONS, AND THE POLICE WOULD JUMP TO THE IMMEDIATE CONCLUSION HE WAS GUILTY.

I MUST MOVE YOU, MY DEAR, BUT JUST UNTIL I GET THIS SORTED OUT.
I *WILL* FIND OUT WHO KILLED YOU.

EVEN IF IT WAS *ME!*

BUT WALTER'S TIME WAS RUNNING OUT FASTER THAN HE REALIZED.
WARRANT

AH, THE NEXT GREAT AMERICAN NOVELIST, HARD AT WORK.
HI, GENE!

DID MY MOM TELL YOU I WAS WRITING A STORY?

I JUST FIGURED THAT GLEAM IN YOUR EYE WAS YOUR IMAGINATION AT WORK.

MY EMMY USED TO GET THAT LOOK IN HER EYES WHEN SHE WOULD WRITE STORIES.
I'M WRITING A MYSTERY.

A ***MURDER*** MYSTERY.

OH, I ENJOY A GOOD MYSTERY. WHAT'S YOURS ABOUT?
IT'S ALL ABOUT WHAT HAPPENED AT THE GOLDSWORTH HOUSE.

OH REALLY?

YEAH, MOM TOLD ME GOLDSWORTH AND HIS WIFE DISAPPEARED THIRTY YEARS AGO AFTER A PARTY THERE.

SO IN MY STORY, ANGELA GOT MURDERED AT THE PARTY, AND WALTER IS THE PRIME SUSPECT!

HMM. SOUNDS LIKE AN INTERESTING STORY.
I'M JUST MAKING UP THE DETAILS. I HAVE NO IDEA WHAT ACTUALLY HAPPENED OF COURSE.

WELL, I'D LOVE TO READ IT WHEN IT'S DONE.
SURE.

OH, HERE COMES SIMON. I TOLD HIM WE COULD GO ON THE LAKE AFTER I WROTE FOR A BIT.

YOU KIDS HAVE FUN!

GOING OUT ON THE WATER?
YEAH.
HEY, YOU SHOULD INVITE THE NEIGHBOR KIDS!

OH COME ON. THEY WOULD PROBABLY LOVE TO EXPLORE WITH YOU.

THEY DON'T EVEN LIKE THE WATER.

THAT CAN'T BE TRUE. EVERYONE LIKES THE WATER.
NO, REALLY, THEY HATE EVERYTHING.

THEY DON'T SEEM THAT BAD. YOU SHOULD INVITE THEM.
DO WE HAVE TO?

OF COURSE YOU DON'T HAVE TO...
GOOD.
...BUT YOU SHOULD.

THAT BASICALLY MEANS WE HAVE TO.

THEY WON'T COME, BUT I GUESS WE CAN ASK.

KNOCK
KNOCK

CLICK
CLICK
CLICK

YES, HELLO?

OH, YOU'RE THE NEIGHBOR KIDS, AREN'T YOU?
YEAH.

WE WERE WONDERING IF PAIGE AND BRYAN WANTED TO GO ON THE LAKE WITH US?

THAT'S A FABULOUS IDEA! THEY'VE BEEN WATCHING TV ALL DAY.
COME ON INSIDE.

PAIGE! BRYAN!
THE NEIGHBOR KIDS ARE HERE!

PAIGE! BRYAN!

GEEZ, CALM DOWN, MOM.
YOU KIDS HAVE FUN!

WHAT'S UP?

NUDGE

UM, DID YOU GUYS WANT TO GO ON THE LAKE WITH US?

EW, SWIMMING?

NO, ON BOATS.

WE HAVE A CANOE AND TWO KAYAKS.
OH.

OKAY SURE, WE'LL GO.
SHRUG

REALLY? LIKE UM, RIGHT NOW?

YEAH, YOU JUST INVITED US, DIDN'T YOU?
LET'S GO!

SO, HAVE YOU GUYS EVER GONE CANOEING BEFORE?

OH NO, WE ACTUALLY NEVER USED OUR ARMS OR LEGS BEFORE THIS TRIP.

SARCASM, RIGHT?
SHE LEARNS!

I CLAIM A KAYAK!
ME TOO!

GUESS WE'RE CANOE BUDDIES.
OH JOY.

OKAY, WE HAVE TO WEAR THESE LIFE JACKETS.
LIFE JACKETS ARE FOR NERDS!
WELL THAT SUITS YOU, THEN, BRYAN.

I'M NOT A NERD -- YOU ARE!

IT'S OKAY, WE CAN ALL BE NERDS TOGETHER!
YOU'RE THE NERD. YOU READ *STAR TREK* BOOKS.
SHUT UP, NERD KING.

IF I'M THE NERD KING, I RULE OVER YOU!

I CAN'T STAND MY BROTHER.
SPLASH!

DO YOU REALLY READ *STAR TREK* BOOKS?
EW, NO.

WOW, LOOK AT THAT FISH JUMP, IT'S HUGE!
WHOA, LOOK AT THOSE DUCKS FIGHTING!
CRAZY, I FEEL LIKE I'M GONNA TIP OVER, BUT I DON'T!

SHUT UP, BRYAN! CAN'T WE JUST BE QUIET AND ENJOY NATURE?

SO, WHAT DO YOUR PARENTS DO FOR A LIVING?
UM, THEY'RE ACCOUNTANTS. EXCITING, RIGHT?

DO THEY DO, LIKE, TAXES AND STUFF?

WHY ARE YOU SO INTERESTED?

I'M JUST TRYING TO MAKE CONVERSATION.

OKAY, RIGHT. SORRY.
YEAH, THEY DO TAXES. HOW ABOUT YOURS?

MY MOM'S A TEACHER, AND MY DAD WORKS AT A PAPER MILL.
OH.

THAT'S NICE.

HEY, THIS IS THE HOUSE WITH THE GATE WE SAW FROM THE ROAD.
OH. HMM.

IT'S FANCY, BUT THERE'S SOMETHING **CREEPY** ABOUT IT.

I WONDER HOW MANY PEOPLE HAVE BEEN MURDERED IN THERE.

IT'S SO WEIRD YOU SAY THAT...THAT'S WHAT MY STORY IS ABOUT!
THE ONE YOU WOULDN'T LET ME READ?
FOR REAL, IT'S ABOUT THIS PLACE?

YEP!
AND MURDER?
COLD BLOODED.

WOW, AGATHA PRISSY! I WOULDN'T HAVE GUESSED YOU HAD IT IN YOU!

WELL LOOK AT THE PLACE. IT HAS MURDER WRITTEN ALL OVER IT!
TOTALLY.

HAVE YOU EVER BEEN INSIDE?

NOPE.

HOW CAN YOU WRITE ABOUT IT IF YOU'VE NEVER BEEN INSIDE?

UM, WITH MY IMAGINATION?

OKAY, WELL CAN I READ IT NOW? I MEAN, IT'S JUST AS MUCH MY IDEA AS YOURS.
IT IS NOT!
CALM DOWN, I WAS KIDDING.

SO, CAN I READ IT?

OKAY, YOU BETTER NOT SHOW ANYONE ELSE.

WHO WOULD I SHOW? MY BROTHER?

I DOUBT HE CAN EVEN READ!
WHERE ARE YOU GUYS GOING?

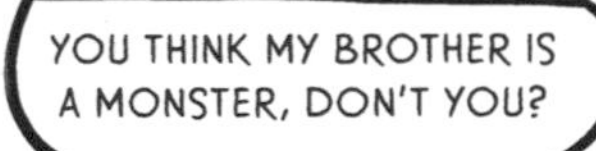

BRYAN MIGHT BE A JERK, BUT HE'S NOT CRUEL TO ANIMALS.

HE SECRETLY LOVES THEM.

LATER
BRYAN AND I FOUND A GIANT EGG SAC TODAY.

ON THE LAKE?
YEAH, IT WAS DISGUSTING. IT LOOKED LIKE A GIANT SNOT BALL!

SIMON, WE'RE EATING.
WE'RE NOT EATING SNOT!

SOUNDS LIKE YOU HAD A LOT OF FUN. GABBY, DID YOU AND PAIGE FIND ANYTHING?

NO, SHE MOSTLY JUST COMPLAINED ABOUT HER FAMILY.

LOOK ON THE BRIGHT SIDE, I SPENT ALL MORNING WRITING MY SCHOLARSHIP ESSAY.

GABBY WOULD PROBABLY ENJOY THAT!

MORE THAN POKING AT EGG SACS, YEAH.

CLICK
CLICK

NOD

AHEM.

KIDS...

YOUR MOM AND I HAVE SOME NEWS TO SHARE WITH YOU.

OH NO.
WHAT'S WRONG?

NO, IT'S NOT BAD NEWS. BUT IT WILL MEAN SOME CHANGES FOR US.

I'M BEING TRANSFERRED.

TRANSFERRED?

THEY'RE CLOSING OUR MILL.
I'M FORTUNATE I STILL HAVE A JOB. A LOT OF PEOPLE WERE LAID OFF.

DOES THAT MEAN WE HAVE TO MOVE?

YES, WE WILL HAVE TO MOVE.

...TO WHERE?

THEY HAVEN'T TOLD ME YET.
THERE ARE MILLS IN A FEW DIFFERENT CITIES. THE MAIN ONE IS IN GEORGIA.

THEY TALK FUNNY IN GEORGIA.

WHAT ABOUT *ME?*
I PICKED A COLLEGE THREE HOURS AWAY FROM HOME. NOW YOU'RE MOVING A THOUSAND MILES AWAY?
HONEY, WE DON'T KNOW THAT.

THIS SUCKS.

WHERE WILL GABBY AND I GO TO SCHOOL?

YOU'LL HAVE A NEW SCHOOL. IT WILL BE AN ADVENTURE!

OKAY, BUT WHAT ABOUT THE COTTAGE? CAN WE STILL COME HERE IN THE SUMMERS?

I DON'T KNOW, SWEETHEART. IF WE HAVE TO MOVE VERY FAR IT WOULD BE HARDER TO VISIT THE COTTAGE.

IT TAKES A LOT OF TIME AND MONEY TO MAINTAIN A PLACE LIKE THIS.

BUT WE COULD STILL COME SOMETIMES, COULDN'T WE?

IT'S EASY TO DRIVE HERE WHEN IT'S JUST A FEW HOURS FROM HOME...

...BUT IF WE HAVE TO MOVE TO ANOTHER PART OF THE COUNTRY IT WOULD BE EXPENSIVE TO TRAVEL AS OFTEN AS WE NEED TO.
BUT WE COULD AT LEAST COME LIKE ONCE A YEAR, RIGHT?

GABBY, THERE'S A GOOD CHANCE WE WILL HAVE TO SELL THE COTTAGE.

NO! WE CAN'T SELL IT! IT'S BEEN IN THE FAMILY SINCE FOREVER!

WE'RE NOT HAPPY ABOUT IT EITHER.
CAN'T YOU GET A DIFFERENT JOB, DAD?
I WISH IT WERE THAT EASY.

YOU SAID THIS WASN'T BAD NEWS, BUT THIS *IS* BAD NEWS.
GABBY, I JUST MEANT --

IF YOU DON'T THINK SELLING THE COTTAGE IS BAD NEWS, THEN YOU DON'T REALLY CARE ABOUT US!

GABBY, LOWER YOUR VOICE.

I JUST THINK IT'S STUPID. YOU'RE BEING SELFISH.
JUST DROP IT, GABBY.

COME ON, GUYS. WE'RE STILL ON VACATION.
THAT'S RIGHT, LET'S ENJOY THE TIME WE HAVE.

LET'S MAKE THE MOST OF THIS WEEK.

I APOLOGIZE FOR MY CAVALIER CHOICE OF WORDS, BUT PLEASE, WALTER, JUST ANSWER THE QUESTION.

GOOD MORNING.
OH HEY.

WHATCHA READING?
YOUR STORY, DUH.

SO UM...WHAT DO YOU THINK?

I MEAN, HONESTLY? IT'S NOT VERY GOOD.

WHAT?
YEAH, WELL...

IT'S BASICALLY JUST A RIP-OFF OF, LIKE, EVERY OTHER MURDER MYSTERY.

NO, IT'S NOT!
THE GUY DOESN'T EVEN KNOW IF HE'S THE MURDERER!

BECAUSE HE DOESN'T REMEMBER! COME ON, THAT'S ORIGINAL.
A KILLER WITH AMNESIA? IT'S BEEN DONE A HUNDRED TIMES.

LET'S BACK UP. WHAT'S HIS MOTIVE?

I DIDN'T FIGURE THAT OUT YET.

THE KILLER HAS TO HAVE A MOTIVE. THAT'S, LIKE, THE MOST BASIC RULE IN MYSTERIES.

YEAH, I KNOW THAT, OBVIOUSLY.

ANYWAY, WHAT DO YOU EVEN KNOW ABOUT WRITING? YOU PROBABLY NEVER EVEN GO TO CLASS!

GEEZ, DON'T GET SO WOUND UP! YOU ASKED ME WHAT I THOUGHT.

IT'S NOT LIKE IT'S ALL BAD. I MEAN, LIKE, THE DETECTIVE CHARACTER IS PRETTY FUNNY.
YEAH?
YEAH, AND WALTER IS KINDA INTERESTING.

BUT YOU NEED MORE DETAILS.
A *LOT* MORE.

A MILLION AND ONE MURDER MYSTERIES ARE SET AT SOME RICH GUY'S HOUSE ON A LAKE.
SO WHY IS THIS ONE *DIFFERENT?*

I WANT MORE DETAILS! WHAT DOES IT LOOK LIKE INSIDE? WHAT DOES IT SMELL LIKE?

WHAT KIND OF ***SINISTER SHADOWS*** DOES THE LIGHT CAST WHEN WALTER DISCOVERS THE BODY?

WHAT KIND OF NOISES KEEP HIM AWAKE AT NIGHT WHILE HE AGONIZES OVER THE POSSIBILITY THAT HE KILLED HIS WIFE?

WHAT HAPPENED THAT NIGHT IN THAT DECADENT LAKE HOUSE, AND WHY?
DO YOU EVEN *KNOW?*

I'M JUST MAKING IT UP AS I GO.
YEAH, IT SHOWS.
NOTES
OKAY, YOU KNOW HOW THEY SAY THAT TO WRITE A GOOD CHARACTER YOU HAVE TO GET INSIDE THEIR HEAD?
WELL, IN YOUR STORY THIS LAKE HOUSE IS A CHARACTER.
WHICH MEANS...
WE HAVE TO GET INSIDE.

WHAT? ***NO WAY!*** SEE, I KNEW YOU WERE CRAZY.

WHAT'S SO CRAZY ABOUT THAT? IT'S CALLED RESEARCH.
IT'S CALLED *TRESPASSING!*
SO?

SO, UM, LET ME SEE... IT'S ILLEGAL!

YOU MIGHT BE USED TO BREAKING THE LAW, BUT I'M NOT.

YOU ASKED ME FOR MY HELP, SO DON'T GO INSULTING ME.

IF YOU'RE HAPPY WITH YOUR BORING STORY, GREAT.
ANY *REAL* ARTIST KNOWS YOU HAVE TO TAKE RISKS TO MAKE ART.

BUT WHAT DO I KNOW? I'M JUST A CRIMINAL, APPARENTLY.

HEY, GABBY!
WE WERE THINKING OF GOING MINI GOLFING TODAY, WHAT DO YOU SAY?

I GUESS.

YOU DON'T SOUND VERY EXCITED.

SURE. LET'S GO HIT A STUPID BALL INTO A STUPID LITTLE HOLE!

Blackbeard
Adventure Golf

ALL RIGHT, SCORES FOR HOLE NUMBER SIX?

FOUR!
THREE FOR ME.
I GOT FOUR.
...FIFTEEN.

YOU'RE NOT EVEN TRYING.
SO?

COME ON, GUYS, MOM'S IN THE LEAD. WE NEED TO CATCH UP!

GOOD LUCK WITH THAT!

HEY, GABBY AND I ARE GONNA HANG BACK A HOLE.
6
HOLE 7

WOULD YOU QUIT ACTING LIKE A BABY?
I'M NOT!

WHAT'S GOING ON WITH YOU?
NOTHING.

YOU'RE BEING IMMATURE AND YOU'RE PUNISHING EVERYONE.
WELL, *SORRY!*

IS THIS ABOUT DAD'S JOB?
NO.
ARE YOU SURE?
DINK

BECAUSE YOU SEEMED PRETTY UPSET ABOUT IT YESTERDAY, AND TODAY YOU'RE BEING A TOTAL BRAT.

NOT TO MENTION YOU'RE PURPOSELY SUCKING AT MINI GOLF.
ZING!
DONK

I KNOW YOU'RE UPSET ABOUT THE TRANSFER. BUT IT'S NOT ALL ABOUT YOU.
YOU THINK THIS DOESN'T AFFECT THE REST OF US TOO? I'M GONNA HAVE TO LOOK AT COLLEGES IN GEORGIA NOW!

BELIEVE IT OR NOT, MOM AND DAD AREN'T TRYING TO RUIN YOUR LIFE, SO JUST GIVE THEM A BREAK, OKAY?

IT'S JUST... STUPID.

I MEAN, THIS COULD BE OUR LAST WEEK AT THE COTTAGE, AND THE DUMB NEIGHBOR KIDS ARE *RUINING* IT.

HOW ARE THEY RUINING IT?
I DUNNO. YOU KNOW PAIGE?

SHE'S RUDE, AND OBNOXIOUS, AND SHE TOLD ME I DON'T KNOW HOW TO WRITE.

OH. SHE HURT YOUR FEELINGS, HUH?
IT'S NOT THAT!

SHE DOESN'T CARE ABOUT ANY OF THE RULES, AND NOW SHE'S TRYING TO GET ME TO BREAK THE RULES.
9
6

BREAK THE RULES HOW?
IT DOESN'T MATTER, I'M NOT GONNA DO IT.
WHAT, SHE DOESN'T WANT YOU TO **MURDER** SOMEONE, DOES SHE?
SLICE!
NO. JUST FORGET IT, MORGAN.

GABBY, DO YOU WANT MY ADVICE?
JUST CALM DOWN ABOUT IT ALL.
BLACK BEARD ADVENTURE GOLF
SNACK BAR
REST ROOMS
6

YOU'RE A SMART KID. YOU'LL KNOW IF PAIGE IS LEADING YOU TO THE DARK SIDE.
SO...YOU THINK I SHOULD DO IT?

I DID **NOT** SAY THAT.
I DON'T EVEN KNOW WHAT KIND OF MISCHIEF YOU'RE TALKING ABOUT.

IT SOUNDS LIKE PAIGE JUST NEEDS A FRIEND.

MAYBE YOU COULD USE ONE TOO?
IT WOULDN'T HURT TO GET OUTSIDE YOUR COMFORT ZONE A LITTLE BIT.

MEANWHILE, COULD YOU PLEASE DROP THE POUTY ACT AND TRY TO HAVE SOME FUN?
6
PLINK
YEAH, FINE.

TINK!

NOW, COME ON, WE CAN'T LET MOM WIN AGAIN OR WE'LL NEVER HEAR THE END OF IT!
7

HEY, I WAS LOOKING ALL OVER FOR YOU.
THOUGHT I'D CHECK OUT THIS INFAMOUS PREGNANT CAT.

YOU'RE NOT GONNA REPORT ME FOR BREAKING AND ENTERING, ARE YOU?

LOOK, ABOUT EARLIER... I'M SORRY. YOU WERE JUST TRYING TO HELP, AND I OVERREACTED.

I SHOULDN'T HAVE CALLED YOU A CRIMINAL MASTERMIND.

YOU NEVER CALLED ME A MASTERMIND. I MIGHT HAVE TAKEN THAT AS A COMPLIMENT.

I GUESS I WAS EXTRA TOUCHY THIS MORNING BECAUSE I FOUND OUT SOME BAD NEWS.
MY DAD'S GETTING TRANSFERRED.
WHAT DOES HE DO AGAIN?

HE'S A MANAGER AT A PAPER MILL. BUT THEY'RE CLOSING IT, SO HE HAS TO GO TO ANOTHER MILL SOMEWHERE.

BUT HE STILL HAS A JOB?
YEAH.

OH. WELL BIG DEAL, THEN.
UM, IT IS A BIG DEAL.

I'M JUST SAYING, IT COULD BE A LOT WORSE.

OKAY. WELL ANYWAY, YOU WERE RIGHT ABOUT MY STORY. IT'S NOT VERY DARING.

AND...
I THINK WE SHOULD BREAK INTO THE GOLDSWORTH HOUSE.
FOR REAL?

WELL, LET ME REPHRASE THAT. I THINK WE SHOULD INVESTIGATE THE PLACE.

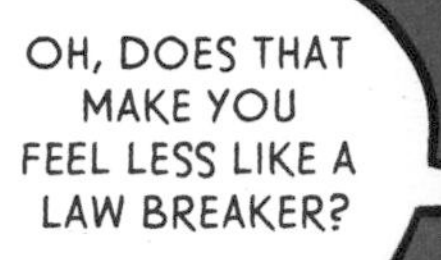

OH, DOES THAT MAKE YOU FEEL LESS LIKE A LAW BREAKER?

EXACTLY, WE'RE JUST BEING DETECTIVES.

WHATEVER IT TAKES TO GET YOU OFF YOUR HIGH HORSE.
VERY FUNNY.

ALSO, I WAS WONDERING IF...MAYBE YOU'D WANT TO HELP ME WRITE MY STORY?
REALLY?

YEAH, WELL, 'CUZ...YOU SEEM LIKE YOU ACTUALLY HAVE SOME PRETTY GOOD IDEAS AND, I DUNNO, IT COULD BE FUN.

OKAY, I'M IN.

SO ARE WE.

WHAT ARE YOU GUYS DOING HERE?
IT'S A FREE COUNTRY!
WE WERE COMING TO FEED THE CAT.

AND WE JUST SO HAPPENED TO OVERHEAR YOUR PLAN TO BREAK INTO THAT MANSION CABIN.

YOU HEARD WRONG. GET LOST.
OH SURE, WE'LL GET LOST.

AND WE'LL TELL MOM AND DAD WHAT YOU'RE PLANNING, AND YOU'LL BE *GROUNDED.*

AND YOU KNOW WHAT THEY SAID ABOUT THE NEXT SCREWUP, PAIGE. IT'S THE BIG ONE.

YOU LITTLE BLACKMAILER.

WELL, I GUESS WE HAVE SOME ACCOMPLICES.
WOO!
YES!

I CAN'T BELIEVE YOU'D GO ALONG WITH THIS, SIMON.
I CAN'T BELIEVE ***YOU*** WOULD!
HOP

LOOKS LIKE YOUR BROTHER IS AS MUCH OF A RAT AS MINE IS.
FOR REAL.

WELL, I VOTE WE GO TONIGHT BEFORE THESE WEENIES BLAB TO OUR PARENTS.
WHICH IS IT, ARE WE RATS OR WEENIES?

YOU GUYS BETTER NOT BE ANY TROUBLE. I'VE GOT DIRT AGAINST YOU TOO, BRYAN. AND IN THIS MISSION, I'M IN CHARGE.

GABBY AND I ARE, I MEAN.

FINE, WHATEVER. NOW, MOVE OVER, WE GOTTA FEED THE CAT!

HERE YOU GO, GIRL. WERE THOSE WEIRD GIRLS BOTHERING YOU?
WHATEVER. SEE YOU, LOSERS.

ALL RIGHT, SEE YOU TONIGHT, I GUESS?
YEAH, I GUESS. LATER.

NO CHICKENING OUT!

OKAY, SIMON. WE'LL NEED TWO FLASHLIGHTS.
THEY'RE IN THE CUPBOARD OVER THE MICROWAVE.
WHERE ARE YOU KIDS OFF TO AT THIS TIME OF NIGHT?

UH...
WE'RE GONNA PLAY GHOST IN THE GRAVEYARD WITH THE NEIGHBORS!
OH, WE USED TO PLAY THAT ALL THE TIME AS KIDS.

HAVE A GOOD TIME!

FAST THINKING!

THERE THEY ARE.
FOR A COUPLE OF REBELS, THEY SURE ARE PUNCTUAL.

READY?

ARE WE GONNA JUMP THE GATE?

NO, WE'LL GO BY WATER SO NO ONE SEES US ON THE ROAD.

GABBY AND I GET THE KAYAKS TONIGHT.
LIKE WE CARE.

EVERYONE STAY CLOSE TOGETHER, OKAY?

SIMON, STAY NEAR ME.

CLUNK! CLANK!
QUIET!

WE'RE SUPPOSED TO HAVE LIGHTS ON OUR BOATS AT NIGHT.

OH RIGHT, 'CUZ THAT WON'T DRAW ATTENTION TO US.

AHH, YOU'RE SPLASHING WATER ON ME!
THAT'S FREAKING COLD!
HA-HA, SORRY!
GUYS, QUIET DOWN!
SERIOUSLY, BRYAN, SHUT UP!

SHUFF
CLUNK

HUSTLE UP, BRYAN! IF ANYONE FALLS, WE'RE *NOT* STOPPING FOR THEM.

YOU'RE RUTHLESS.
I HAVE TO BE. BRYAN THINKS EVERYTHING IS A JOKE.

THERE IT IS...

ARE YOU SURE YOU WANT TO DO THIS, SIMON?
UH, YEAH... TOTALLY.
I'M NOT.

OKAY, NOW WE HAVE TO FIGURE OUT HOW TO GET INSIDE.

THROUGH THE WINDOW!

NO, WE'RE NOT TRYING TO GET BUSTED, YOU MORON.

BRYAN, SIMON, YOU TWO GO TO THE FRONT AND LOOK FOR A KEY.
LOOK FOR ANY SUSPICIOUS-LOOKING ROCKS OR CERAMIC TURTLES NEARBY.
THAT'S AN OBVIOUS "HIDE-A-KEY."

AND PUT YOUR HOODS UP IF YOU SEE ANY SECURITY CAMERAS!
DONE THIS BEFORE?

WHAT DO WE DO?
LET'S CHECK THE WINDOWS...

IF THIS PLACE WAS ABANDONED IN A HURRY, MAYBE THEY FORGOT TO LOCK ONE.

UFF. NO LUCK HERE.
HERE EITHER.

I DON'T THINK THESE WINDOWS EVEN OPEN.
HEY, THERE'S A STAIRCASE OVER HERE!

I FOUND A DOOR!
THAT WILL FOR SURE BE LOCKED.

CLICK!

I CAN'T BELIEVE THAT ACTUALLY WORKED!
I HAVE SOME TRICKS TOO!

FLICK
ON
FLICK
FLICK

CLICK

THUD THUD THUD

WE FOUND A KEY!

IT WAS UNLOCKED.
OH.

WE BROKE IN!
SLAP

OKAY, NOBODY *TOUCH* ANYTHING. AND DEFINITELY DON'T *TAKE* ANYTHING!
AW MAN, WHAT ARE WE EVEN HERE FOR, THEN?

WE'RE JUST LOOKING AROUND, GATHERING INTELLIGENCE.

NO INTELLIGENCE HERE!
AHH! QUIT IT, BRYAN!

CAN WE SPLIT UP?
NO!

MAYBE WE SHOULD. THESE GUYS ARE ONLY GONNA GET IN THE WAY.

NO WAY. WE'RE STICKING TOGETHER.
FINE. LAME.

WHAT'S SO GREAT ABOUT THIS PLACE ANYWAY?
EVER HEARD OF WALTER GOLDSWORTH?
NOPE.

I GUESS HE WAS A PRETTY FAMOUS ARCHITECT BACK IN THE DAY.
BORING.

WELL, WALTER USED TO LIVE HERE, AND ONE DAY HE JUST DISAPPEARED, ALONG WITH HIS WIFE.
CLICK

AND I THINK HE MURDERED HER HERE.

WHOA!

GEEZ, THE MOON IS SO BRIGHT IT'S PRACTICALLY DAY!
GUESS WE WON'T NEED FLASHLIGHTS.
CLICK

SO, WHAT ARE WE LOOKING FOR EXACTLY?
EVIDENCE? A BODY??
NO, JUST... INSPIRATION.

OH. YAWN.
SHUT UP, BRYAN.

IF THERE WAS A MURDER HERE IT WOULD HAVE HAPPENED A LONG TIME AGO.

THEY NEVER FOUND WALTER OR HIS WIFE, SO I DOUBT WE WILL EITHER.

SO, WE'RE JUST...
TRYING TO IMAGINE WHAT MIGHT HAVE HAPPENED HERE.

THAT SOUNDS **SO** BORING. CAN WE PLEASE GO EXPLORE A LITTLE?
WE WON'T GO FAR.
FINE.

YOU BETTER COME WHEN I CALL YOU!
WE WILL!
AND DON'T STEAL ANYTHING!

CAN YOU BELIEVE THIS PLACE, PAIGE?
IT'S WILD.

SOMETHING *DEFINITELY* HAPPENED HERE. SOMETHING TRAGIC.
I CAN JUST FEEL IT.

YOU THINK THIS WALTER GUY REALLY *DID* KILL HIS WIFE?

I DON'T KNOW. THAT'S WHAT WE HAVE TO FIGURE OUT.

AND LIKE YOU SAID, WE HAVE TO START WITH A MOTIVE.

HOW COULD YOU LIVE IN A HOUSE THIS COOL AND WANT TO KILL SOMEONE?
YEAH, LET ALONE YOUR BABE OF A WIFE?

MY MOM SAID SOMETHING WAS GOING ON WITH THEM.
MAYBE THEIR MARRIAGE WASN'T SO GREAT? MAYBE THEY WERE FIGHTING A LOT?

MY PARENTS FIGHT ALL THE TIME, BUT I DON'T THINK THEY'D ***KILL*** EACH OTHER.

OKAY, LET'S START FROM ANOTHER ANGLE. WHY DID THEY LEAVE CHICAGO?
THEY BOTH HAD SUCCESSFUL CAREERS. HE'S A HOTSHOT ARCHITECT, SHE'S A FASHION MODEL...
WHY MOVE UP HERE TO THE WOODS?
MAYBE THEY WERE DRIVEN OUT OF TOWN BY THE PAPARAZZI.

THEY WERE SUPER FAMOUS, RIGHT?
FAMOUS ENOUGH THAT THE LOCAL PAPER WROTE ABOUT THEM MOVING HERE.
OKAY, WHAT ABOUT THIS...

OF COURSE THEY FOUGHT.

WHY MUST YOU RUIN MY HAPPINESS?

DON'T BE SO MELODRAMATIC.

ARE YOU JEALOUS OF MY ADORING FANS OR JUST MY **SUCCESS?**

MAYBE IF YOU PAID ME **HALF** THE ATTENTION THAT YOU DO TO YOUR WORK!

LET'S LOOK AROUND MORE.

OKAY, SO, WHAT ABOUT THIS PARTY? WHOSE IDEA WAS *THAT?*

PROBABLY ANGELA'S IF SHE WAS MISSING HER CHICAGO PEOPLE.

SO WHY WOULD WALTER AGREE TO IT...

EW, THAT'S DISGUSTING, DO YOU KNOW HOW OLD THAT PIPE IS?

I THOUGHT WE WEREN'T GONNA TOUCH ANYTHING.
GEEZ, EVEN WHEN YOU'RE BREAKING THE LAW YOU'RE NO FUN.

HOLY CRAP!

GABBY, I HAVE OUR MOTIVE!

WALTER ISN'T JEALOUS OF HER CAREER, HE'S JUST JEALOUS.
HE THINKS ANGELA IS CHEATING ON HIM!

WHY WOULD A LIGHTER MEAN SHE'S CHEATING ON HIM?
Flick

IT COULD BE WALTER'S. HECK, IT COULD BE HERS!

LOOK CLOSER. IT'S ENGRAVED.

WHO IS E.H.?
IT'S NOT WALTER GOLDSWORTH, THAT'S FOR SURE!

YOU'RE RIGHT!
E.H. WHO KNOWS... IT MUST'VE BEEN SOMEONE FROM CHICAGO. THAT'S WHY WALTER MOVED THEM UP HERE.
AND WHY SHE DIDN'T WANT TO GO.

SHE WAS HAVING AN *AFFAIR.*
AND GOLDSWORTH WAS ONTO IT.

GENIUS!

BUT HE'S NOT SURE EXACTLY WHO IT IS.
YEAH, SO THAT'S WHY WALTER DECIDES TO THROW THIS PARTY.

HE INVITES EVERYONE THEY KNOW FROM CHICAGO, KNOWING THAT ANGELA'S *FLING* WILL SHOW UP AND HE CAN CATCH THEM TOGETHER.
AND WHEN HE DOES...*HE'LL KILL THEM!*

WE HAVE OUR MOTIVE!

CRASH!!!

Ohhhh...

Oww...

BRYAN!
Oww

WHAT HAPPENED??
THIS DUMB THING TIPPED OVER ON ME!

I **TOLD** YOU NOT TO TOUCH ANYTHING.

WE DIDN'T!

ARE YOU OKAY?

I THINK I BROKE MY WRIST!
OH NO!

HOW DID THIS HAPPEN?

I DON'T KNOW! WE WERE JUST WALKING AROUND.
Shrug

MY LEG GOT TANGLED IN ONE OF THESE STUPID SHEETS AND IT PULLED THIS BOOKCASE OVER AND KNOCKED ME DOWN.

LET ME SEE.
OW!
SORRY! IT DOES LOOK SWOLLEN.

YEAH, DUH, I JUST GOT SQUISHED, REMEMBER?

WE HAVE TO GO GET HELP.
NO!

IF MY MOM AND DAD FIND OUT ABOUT THIS I'M *DEAD.*

WE HAVE TO GET OUT OF HERE.

BRYAN, CAN YOU GET UP?

GROAN
YEAH.

DO YOU THINK YOU CAN PADDLE?

I DON'T THINK SO.

I CAN PADDLE THE CANOE. HE CAN JUST RIDE ALONG.
GREAT, LET'S GO!

WHAT ARE WE SUPPOSED TO TELL OUR PARENTS?
I DUNNO, MAKE SOMETHING UP!
TELL THEM BRYAN TRIPPED DURING OUR GAME.

HE PROBABLY WOULD HAVE ANYWAY.
OH, *REAL NICE,* PAIGE!

PAIGE, I DON'T LIKE LYING TO MY PARENTS.
GABBY, PLEASE.

I CAN'T GET *BUSTED* FOR THIS.

YOU KEEP SAYING THAT. WHAT'S GONNA HAPPEN? WILL THEY SEND YOU OFF TO BOARDING SCHOOL OR SOMETHING?
EVEN *WORSE.*
EVER HEARD OF PEORIA?

YEAH, I THINK SO. THAT'S IN ILLINOIS, RIGHT?

YEAH, RIGHT SMACK IN THE MIDDLE OF ILLINOIS.
TWO AND A HALF MISERABLE HOURS FROM CHICAGO.
BRYAN, BE CAREFUL!

OKAY...SO?
SO MY MOM IS ALWAYS THREATENING ME...

...THAT IF I DON'T BEHAVE SHE'S GONNA SEND ME TO LIVE WITH HER CRAZY AUNT IN PEORIA.

THAT'S IT? I THOUGHT YOU SAID YOUR PARENTS WERE GONNA KILL YOU!
GEEZ, YOU TAKE EVERYTHING SO LITERALLY!

AND ANYWAY, YOU HAVEN'T MET THIS WOMAN. I THINK I'D RATHER BE MURDERED THAN LIVE WITH MY NEENAW.

SHE DRESSES HER DOGS LIKE POP STARS AND ENTERS THEM IN COMPETITIONS. GUESS WHO'D BE ON PERMANENT GROOMING DUTY?
THAT'S RIGHT. ME!

IMAGINE GETTING TWO SQUIRMY POMERANIANS INTO SPANDEX JUMPSUITS EVERY WEEKEND.
THAT WOULD BE MY LIFE.

THAT DOESN'T SOUND SO BAD.

LOOK, THE POINT IS, MY PARENTS DON'T EVEN WANT ME AROUND ANYMORE.

SO ANY EXCUSE THEY CAN USE TO SHIP ME OFF, THEY ARE GONNA TAKE IT.
I'M SURE THAT'S NOT TRUE.

WHAT, THAT MY PARENTS HATE ME? THAT I DON'T HAVE ANY ROOM TO MESS UP?

NOT EVERYONE LIVES IN A PERFECT LITTLE FAMILY BUBBLE LIKE YOU DO.

I DON'T LIVE IN A BUBBLE.

NO? THEN YOU WON'T MIND LYING TO YOUR PARENTS ABOUT THIS.

WHERE ARE MOM AND DAD?
THEY WENT INTO TOWN.
DAD SAID THE PONTOON NEEDED GAS.

Jump!

WANNA PLAY FRISBEE?
NO THANKS.

WHAT ELSE ARE YOU GONNA DO? WRITE YOUR DUMB STORY?
NONE OF YOUR BUSINESS.

LET'S SEE IT!
SNATCH!
GIVE THAT BACK!

"DETECTIVE LONGLEY CRADLED THE SMALL CHROME LIGHTER IN THE PALM OF HIS HAND."

"HE HADN'T KNOWN WALTER GOLDSWORTH TO BE A SMOKER, BUT HE HADN'T KNOWN HIM TO BE VIOLENT EITHER."
"YET HERE HE WAS INVESTIGATING THE DISAPPEARANCE AND POSSIBLE MURDER OF WALTER'S WIFE."

KNOCK IT OFF, YOU BUTTHEAD!
MORGAN, CATCH!

CATCH!

"THE LIGHTER WAS A CLUE, CERTAINLY, BUT TO WHAT, EXACTLY?"
"THAT WALTER WAS FILLING HIS LUNGS WITH SMOKE WHEN NO ONE WAS LOOKING?"
"UNHEALTHY BEHAVIOR, BUT NOT A CRIME."

"NO, THE GREATER CLUE WERE THE LETTERS ETCHED INTO THE LIGHTER: 'E.H.' ANOTHER PLAYER IN THIS BLOODTHIRSTY GAME. ANOTHER STEP CLOSER TO THE TRUTH."

GIVE IT ***BACK!***
SNATCH

OH COME ON, WE'RE JUST MESSING AROUND. IT SOUNDS REALLY GOOD!
YEAH, WHAT HAPPENS NEXT?

SWISH

I THOUGHT YOU HATED SPORTS.

I DO. BUT IT'S THE LEAST WORST THING TO DO HERE.

HOW'S YOUR BROTHER?
HE'S FINE.

HE SPRAINED HIS WRIST BUT DIDN'T HAVE TO GO TO THE DOCTOR. HE'S JUST ICING IT.
OH GOOD.

WERE YOUR PARENTS MAD?

NO, THEY WERE JUST GLAD WE WERE HANGING OUT WITH YOU GUYS.

THEY THINK YOU'RE SUCH GOOD KIDS.

SO WHAT ARE YOU DOING TODAY?

I DUNNO. PLAYING SOME BASKETBALL, I GUESS.

WANT TO GO BACK?

BACK TO...

TO THE GOLDSWORTH HOUSE, *DUH.*

UM, ARE YOU *CRAZY?*

DID YOU FORGET WHAT HAPPENED LAST NIGHT?
WHAT, CRASHING OVER FURNITURE AND RUNNING FOR OUR LIVES?
EXACTLY!

COME ON, GABBY.
YOU KNOW YOU WANT TO FIGURE OUT WHAT REALLY HAPPENED THERE.

I THOUGHT YOU WERE WORRIED ABOUT GETTING SENT TO YOUR AUNT'S HOUSE OR WHATEVER.

BONK

WELL YEAH, BUT THAT'S ONLY IF WE GET CAUGHT.
REBOUND!

WE WON'T BRING OUR DUMB BROTHERS THIS TIME.
THEY'RE THE BONEHEADS WHO ALMOST BLEW IT.
I DUNNO...

LOOK, WE HAVE TO GO BACK AND PICK UP THE BOOKCASE AND ALL THOSE BOOKS, AT THE VERY LEAST.

OTHERWISE SOMEONE WILL SEE THERE WAS A BREAK-IN, THEY'LL DUST FOR FINGERPRINTS...
AND WE'LL GO TO *JAIL.*

NO, WE WOULDN'T.

WOULD WE?

OF COURSE NOT.

BUT I KNOW YOU WANT THE REAL STORY.

SIGH OKAY. WHEN DO WE GO?

AS SOON AS I MAKE THIS SHOT.

SWISH

AFTERNOON, GIRLS. WHAT ARE YOU UP TO?

UH...WE'RE WORKING ON MY STORY. PAIGE IS HELPING ME NOW.
AH. YOU'VE RECRUITED AN *EXPERT.*

AN EXPERT?

WELL YOU KNOW, SINCE PAIGE IS --
SUCH A GOOD WRITER.
OBVIOUSLY.

AH, YES. THAT'S EXACTLY WHAT I MEANT.
OKAY...
WHAT ARE YOU DOING TODAY, GENE?

I'M HEADING INTO TOWN FOR BINGO.

EVERY WEDNESDAY AND FRIDAY!
I KNOW IT'S CLICHÉD BUT DOGGONE IF IT AIN'T FUN.

HOPE YOU WIN BIG!
HERE'S HOPING! YOU GIRLS HAVE FUN!

WHY'D HE CALL YOU AN EXPERT?
WHO KNOWS.

THAT GUY IS A LITTLE WEIRD, ISN'T HE?

NO WAY, GENE IS THE NICEST!

I BET HE GOES TO BINGO TO MEET ALL THE OLD LADIES.

HE'S A WIDOWER!

EXACTLY. HE'S BACK ON THE *PROWL.*

NO WAY, GENE LOVED HIS WIFE TOO MUCH FOR THAT.

SHE WAS SO SWEET AND HE WAS SUPER DEPRESSED AT HER FUNERAL.
YEAH, WELL, YOU KNOW WHAT THEY SAY...

THERE'S NO BETTER CURE FOR A BROKEN HEART THAN THE HOT OLD LADIES AT THE BINGO HALL.

YOU'RE TERRIBLE!

PRETTY SWEET OLD TRUCK HE'S GOT ANYWAY.

YEAH, DON'T GET ANY IDEAS.
WHAT?

OH PLEASE.
YOUR FACE HAS "JOYRIDE" WRITTEN ALL OVER IT!

YOU DON'T HAVE TO BROADCAST OUR ARRIVAL TO THE WHOLE LAKE.

YOU WANTED TO COME BACK HERE, SO YOU CAN'T COMPLAIN.

OKAY, SO...

WALTER THINKS ANGELA HAS BEEN CHEATING ON HIM WITH ONE OF HER DESIGNERS IN CHICAGO.

SOME GUY E.H., WHO FOR THE SAKE OF OUR STORY WE'RE CALLING EDDIE HAMILTON.
YEAH. AND WALTER'S FURIOUS.

BY THE TIME OF THE PARTY, HE'S SUPER PARANOID AND ANGRY.
AND HE'S PREPARED TO KILL THEM BOTH IF HE FINDS ANYTHING.

'KAY, WAIT, LET ME GET THIS DOWN...

ON THE NIGHT OF THE PARTY, THE HOUSE IS FILLED WITH GUESTS. EVERYONE IS SWAYING TO THE SOUND OF JAZZ AND WAVING THEIR DRINKS AROUND WHILE THEY TALK.

GOLDSWORTH STANDS AT THE BAR, FILLED WITH SUSPICION.

ANGELA, ON THE OTHER HAND, IS THE LIFE OF THE PARTY.

AT THIS POINT I FEEL NO OBLIGATION TO EXPLAIN MYSELF TO YOU.
HAVE YOU *EVER?*
I'M GOING TO KEEP ENTERTAINING. *ONE OF US* HAS TO.
PLEASE, DON'T LET ME STOP YOU!
SLAM

WHY DO WE HAVE TO GO IN THE SUPPLY CLOSET, PAIGE?

TO LOOK FOR A MURDER WEAPON. OBVIOUSLY.

WE CAN RULE OUT A GUN OR ANYTHING VERY LOUD.
WHY?

BECAUSE NO ONE AT THE PARTY REPORTED HEARING ANYTHING OUT OF THE ORDINARY.

IT HAD TO BE SOMETHING QUIETER.

LIKE A KNIFE, OR POISON, OR...

MARBLE CLOCK?

WHAT? THEY USED IT IN *AND THEN THERE WERE NONE.*

ACTUALLY...

DOESN'T SOMEONE GET STRANGLED IN THAT BOOK?

IT WOULD BE QUIET.
YIKES!

THAT'S SO BRUTAL.
I MEAN, IT'S *MURDER.* THERE'S NOT REALLY A NICE WAY TO DO IT.

BUT SOMETHING STILL FEELS LIKE IT'S MISSING.
THERE *HAD* TO BE SOMEONE ELSE INVOLVED.
EDDIE HAMILTON, RIGHT?

I DON'T KNOW. SOMETHING ABOUT THAT JUST DOESN'T FEEL RIGHT. I MEAN, WE JUST *INVENTED* THAT GUY.

WELL, I'M STUCK.

LET'S GO CLEAN UP THE BOOKCASE. MAYBE WALKING AROUND WILL HELP.

ONE, TWO, THREE, LIFT!

THIS THING IS HEAVY!

I BET YOU ANYTHING THAT BRYAN DIDN'T JUST "TRIP ON A SHEET."

DESIGN
MODERN ARCHITECTURE in the POST MODERN WORLD
DESIGN FOR THE EARTH
CRAFT is ART

ELEMENTS OF MODERN DESIGN... PHILOSOPHY OF ORGANIC ARCHITECTURE...

I GUESS THESE ARE THE KINDS OF BOOKS YOU'D EXPECT AN ARCHITECT TO HAVE.

DUDE HAS A LOT OF SCIENCE FICTION TOO.
WAR OF THE WORLDS

PHOTOS

HEY, HERE'S A PHOTO OF HIM WHEN HE WAS YOUNGER!

WRIGHT HALL
HE MUST BE A STUDENT HERE.

LOOK AT THAT ONE.

GUESS HE LIKED DOGS.

HEY, THERE'S ONE WITH ANGELA.
SHE LOOKS PRETTY DOWN-TO-EARTH HERE.

WHO'S THIS OTHER GUY?
PHOTOS

OH MY GOSH...

THAT'S *GENE!*

GENE?
YEAH, OUR NEIGHBOR.

WAIT, REALLY?
PHOTOS
HE'S SO YOUNG!

WE JUST SAW HIM LEAVE FOR BINGO?

I GUESS IT'S AN OLD PHOTO, SO THAT MAKES SENSE.

YEAH, AND GENE ALREADY LIVED THERE WHEN MY MOM WAS A LITTLE GIRL, SO THE TIME FRAME FITS.

I THOUGHT WALTER WAS A TOTAL RECLUSE THOUGH.

WELL, WE JUST MADE THAT PART UP. I GUESS WE WERE WRONG ABOUT THAT.
HMM. SO GOLDSWORTH HAS A FRIEND.

WAIT, LOOK AT THIS.
PHOTOS

LOOK AT GENE'S EYES.
PHOTOS

WHAT ABOUT THEM?

HE'S NOT LOOKING AT THE CAMERA...

HE'S LOOKING AT ANGELA.
HE IS?

HOLY CRAP, GABBY...

ANGELA WAS HAVING AN AFFAIR WITH GENE!

WHAT?!

IT WASN'T SOME FANCY CHICAGO FASHION DESIGNER AT ALL, IT WAS A GOOD OL' LOCAL BOY!

NO WAY, THAT WOULD NEVER HAPPEN. GENE IS AN HONEST, NICE PERSON.

THAT'S WHY GOLDSWORTH NEVER SUSPECTED IT!

HE KNEW ANGELA WASN'T BEING FAITHFUL BUT ASSUMED IT WAS SOMEONE FROM CHICAGO, NOT HIS NEW BEST FRIEND.

"E.H." GABBY, THINK ABOUT IT.
GENE IS SHORT FOR *EUGENE!*

WHAT'S HIS LAST NAME?

HENDERSON.
SEE?
IT FITS PERFECTLY!

I DUNNO.
COME ON, GABBY.

YOU KNOW IT'S THE BEST THEORY SO FAR.
MAYBE.

WE SHOULD PROBABLY GET GOING.
IT'S GETTING LATE.

SHOULD WE TAKE THIS PHOTO ALBUM? IT'S A GOLD MINE FOR EVIDENCE.
PHOTOS

UM, MAYBE JUST THAT GROUP PHOTO.
JUST TO BORROW.

WHY DON'T YOU HANG ON TO IT. LET IT INSPIRE YOU.

CAN'T BELIEVE I'M ASKING THIS, BUT...
SHOULD WE GO BACK TOMORROW?
WE TOTALLY HAVE TO NOW!

WELL, LOOK WHO IT IS!

THE MYSTERIOUS GABBY WOODS! WHERE HAVE YOU BEEN OFF TO?

WE WERE JUST EXPLORING.
WELL, WE'RE GETTING READY TO ROAST SOME HOT DOGS AND MARSHMALLOWS. HUNGRY?
DUMP
UH, SURE.

I'VE GOT A FOOLPROOF NEW ROASTING METHOD I CAN SHOW YOU.
PERFECTLY GOLDEN EVERY TIME!

I'M NOT TOO LATE, AM I?

I BROUGHT POTATO CHIPS!
CRISPY
CHIPS

GENE! GLAD YOU COULD JOIN US!
HEY THERE, GABBY.
UH, HI.

GABBY, CAN YOU RUN INSIDE AND GRAB THE SKEWERS?
'K.

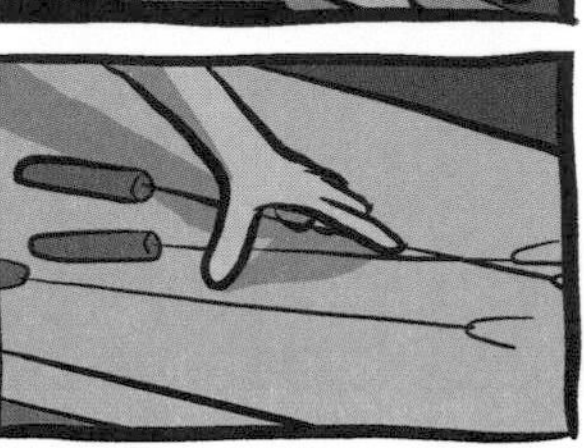

I DON'T THINK I'VE EVER RUN SO FAST IN MY LIFE!
THAT THING CHASED US AT LEAST THREE MILES BEFORE WE REALIZED IT WAS A DOG AND NOT A BEAR!
HA!
HA-HA!

EMMY AND I
DECIDED THAT DAY
WE WERE CAT
PEOPLE!

GENE'S STORIES
ARE THE BEST!

DOES IT HAVE TO BE GENE?

COME ON, LOOK AT THE EVIDENCE.

I KNOW WHAT THE PICTURE LOOKS LIKE, BUT I KNOW HIM IN REAL LIFE AND HE'S NOT LIKE THAT.
YOU DON'T REALLY KNOW THAT THOUGH, DO YOU?

YOU SEE HIM, WHAT, ONE WEEK OUT OF THE YEAR?

YEAH, SO?

PEOPLE CAN SURPRISE YOU!

SHORTLY AFTER HE MOVED TO THE LAKE, WALTER GOLDSWORTH MET EUGENE HENDERSON AND THE TWO BECAME FAST FRIENDS.

ANGELA REMAINED BITTER THAT WALTER HAD MOVED THEM AWAY FROM THEIR HOME IN CHICAGO.

SOON, AFTER SPENDING SO MUCH TIME WITH THE YOUNG COUPLE, GENE FELL IN LOVE WITH ANGELA, DESPITE HIS FRIENDSHIP WITH WALTER.

ANGELA, SEEING HER CHANCE TO GET BACK AT WALTER FOR TAKING HER AWAY FROM CHICAGO, MAKES HER MOVE.

SHE STARTS SEEING GENE ON THE SIDE, THE ULTIMATE BETRAYAL OF HER HUSBAND'S TRUST.

AT FIRST IT'S JUST A GAME. SHE DOESN'T CARE ABOUT GENE, SHE JUST WANTS TO HURT WALTER. BUT EVENTUALLY, AFTER SPENDING TIME WITH HIM, ANGELA FALLS FOR GENE TOO.
DINER

I'M SORRY, I JUST CANNOT IMAGINE GENE DOING *ANY* OF THIS.

WELL ***TRY***.

OKAY, SO...

WALTER SUSPECTS ANGELA IS CHEATING, BUT HE HAS NO IDEA IT'S WITH HIS BEST FRIEND.

ONE DAY HE CONFIDES HIS SUSPICION TO GENE.
I THINK ANGELA'S BEEN RUNNING AROUND ON ME.
YOU... YOU ***DO***?
YEAH, WITH ONE OF HER DESIGNERS. I'M ALMOST CERTAIN.

WELL...WHAT ARE YOU GOING TO DO ABOUT IT?

I'LL TELL YOU WHAT I'M GONNA DO. ANGELA MISSES CHICAGO SO MUCH, WE'LL INVITE *CHICAGO* UP FOR A PARTY.

BUT AT THIS PARTY, I'M GONNA CATCH THEM TOGETHER.
AND IF YOU CATCH THEM -- THEN WHAT?

IF I CATCH THEM... THEN I'M GONNA ***KILL*** THEM.

SO GENE, OF COURSE, HAS TO WARN ANGELA.

COULDN'T WAIT TO SEE ME AGAIN, COULD YOU?

ANGELA, YOU'RE NOT SAFE!
WHAT ARE YOU TALKING ABOUT?

WALTER KNOWS YOU'RE HAVING AN AFFAIR.
GOOD, THAT'S THE WHOLE POINT.

WHAT DO YOU MEAN, THAT'S THE POINT? I THOUGHT YOU *LOVED* ME?

I *DO* LOVE YOU, GENE. AND THAT'S WHY I DON'T CARE IF WALTER FINDS OUT.

IT SERVES HIM RIGHT -- ALL HE LOVES IS THIS *STUPID HOUSE* OF HIS.

HE DOESN'T KNOW IT'S ME. HE THINKS YOU'RE SEEING YOUR DESIGNER.

MY DESIGNER? WHERE ON EARTH DID HE COME UP WITH THAT?

I DON'T KNOW, BUT IT WORKS IN OUR FAVOR. HE DOESN'T *SUSPECT* US!

HE'LL BE SO PREOCCUPIED WITH HIS JEALOUSY AND ANGER AT YOUR DESIGNER, HE'LL NEVER NOTICE IF WE'RE GONE...
WHAT ARE YOU SAYING, GENE...?

YOU CAN ***RUN AWAY*** WITH ME. WE'LL GO TOGETHER. TONIGHT!

YOU'VE LOST YOUR MIND, GENE. WE *CAN'T* RUN AWAY.
YOU'RE ***NOT SAFE*** HERE!

WALTER SAID IF HE CAUGHT YOU WITH SOMEONE TONIGHT HE WOULD **KILL** YOU!

OH, WALTER IS ALWAYS SAYING THINGS LIKE THAT. HE'S A VERY DRAMATIC MAN.
HE SOUNDED DEAD SERIOUS TO ME.

OKAY, THEN IT'S SIMPLE. WE WON'T LET HIM CATCH US.
?

AND IF YOU WON'T RUN AWAY WITH ME, THEN HOW DO YOU PROPOSE WE DO THAT?

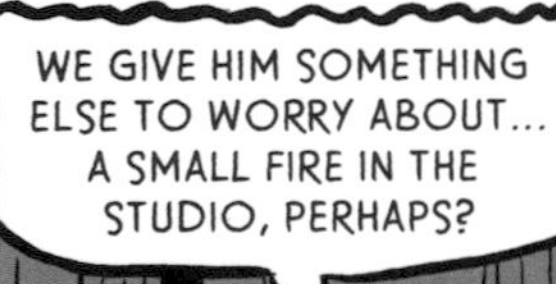
WE GIVE HIM SOMETHING ELSE TO WORRY ABOUT... A SMALL FIRE IN THE STUDIO, PERHAPS?

Flick

AND WHILE HIS FIRST LOVE IS BURNING, BABY, THEN YOU AND ME, WE CAN BE *INVISIBLE.*

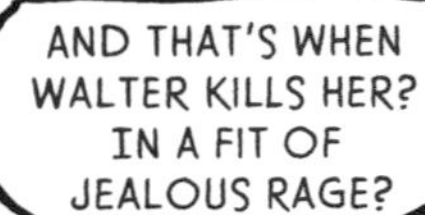
AND THAT'S WHEN WALTER KILLS HER? IN A FIT OF JEALOUS RAGE?

NO, I THINK WALTER WOULD BE MORE METICULOUS THAN THAT.

HIS GUESTS WON'T KNOW WHAT HAPPENED. HE WON'T LEAVE A TRACE.

BUT ANGELA ISN'T GOING TO ESCAPE THE NIGHT WITH HER LIFE!

ARE YOU GETTING ALL THIS?
UH-HUH.
Scribble
Scribble

WALTER HAS THE PERFECT PLAN...
...TO KILL ANGELA, GET RID OF THE BODY, AND GET OUT OF TOWN WITHOUT EVER BEING SEEN.

WHAT ABOUT GENE?
WHAT ABOUT HIM?

WHY DOESN'T WALTER KILL ***HIM*** TOO?

WASN'T THAT PART OF HIS PLAN ALL ALONG? TO KILL ANGELA ***AND*** THE GUY SHE'S BEEN CHEATING WITH?
HMM, YEAH, AND HE'S CLEARLY STILL ALIVE.

AND WHY DOESN'T GENE REPORT WALTER AFTER ANGELA GOES MISSING? HE'S OBVIOUSLY THE *PRIME SUSPECT.*
OKAY, SO WE HAVE A FEW MORE PLOT HOLES TO WORK OUT. BUT --

SLAM

WAS THAT THE FRONT DOOR?
SOUNDED LIKE A CAR DOOR.

WHOA, GABBY...
THAT'S GENE'S TRUCK!

AND THAT'S *DEFINITELY GENE!*

shut

CHOP
CHOP
CHOP
GABBY, WHAT IS HE --
I DON'T KNOW!
SHOULD WE TRY TO GET CLOSER?
NO!
OH MY GOSH, WHAT IS IN THAT BOX?
SHH!

Putta
putta
VROOM

HO-LY-CRAP.

GENE JUST WALKED IN HERE LIKE HE OWNS THE PLACE! DID YOU *SEE* THAT?
UH, DUH, I WAS RIGHT NEXT TO YOU.

SEE, I TOLD YOU HE WAS INVOLVED!

OHMIGOSH, GABBY... WALTER DIDN'T KILL ANGELA...

...***GENE*** DID IT!

WHAT?

THAT IS *TOTALLY* UNBELIEVABLE!

THEN WHY THE HECK IS GENE SNOOPING AROUND IN GOLDSWORTH'S HOUSE ALL THESE YEARS LATER?

THINK ABOUT IT, HE'S STILL COVERING IT UP!
GABBY, HE DIDN'T JUST KILL ANGELA, *HE KILLED WALTER TOO!*

ARE YOU KIDDING ME?

IT MAKES PERFECT SENSE. THAT'S WHY NO BODIES WERE EVER FOUND.

EESH, WHAT DO YOU THINK HE WAS DOING WITH THAT AX?

GENE KNEW THAT ANGELA WOULD NEVER BE HIS AS LONG AS WALTER WAS IN THE PICTURE...

SO ON THE NIGHT OF THE PARTY HE CAME UP WITH A PLAN TO ELIMINATE THE COMPETITION.

BUT THEN THINGS WENT TERRIBLY WRONG.

MY LOVE, YOU'VE SEEN TOO MUCH.

PAIGE, *COME ON.* THERE IS *NO WAY* THAT ANYONE WOULD BELIEVE THAT!

WHY NOT? ARE YOU AND GENE IN SOME KIND OF SAINTHOOD CLUB?

I BET GENE IS AS LIKELY AS ANYONE ELSE TO BE A KILLER.

THERE ARE SO MANY HOLES IN YOUR THEORY I DON'T KNOW WHERE TO BEGIN.

WHY WOULD GENE KILL WALTER IF THEY WERE FRIENDS?
WHY WOULD HE KILL ANGELA IF HE WAS IN LOVE WITH HER?!

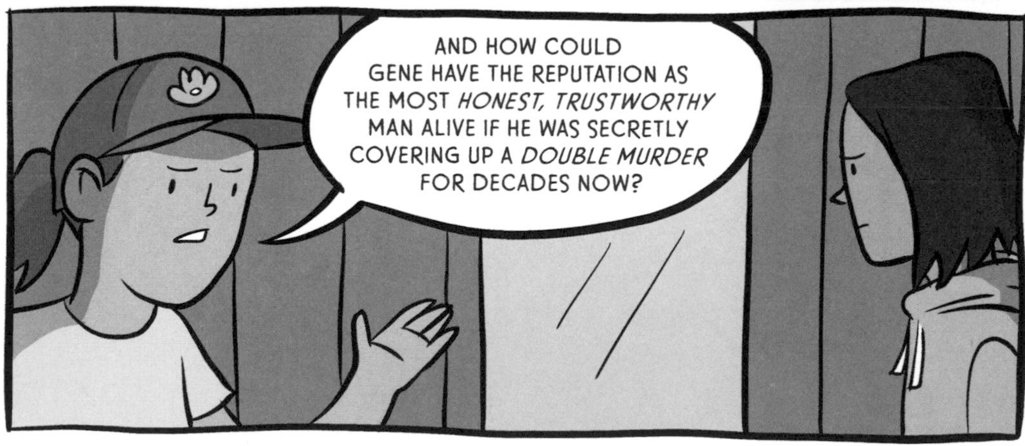
AND HOW COULD GENE HAVE THE REPUTATION AS THE MOST *HONEST, TRUSTWORTHY* MAN ALIVE IF HE WAS SECRETLY COVERING UP A *DOUBLE MURDER* FOR DECADES NOW?

YOU'RE RIGHT, WE DON'T KNOW ENOUGH.
THANK YOU!

WE'LL HAVE TO BREAK INTO GENE'S PLACE NEXT.

WHAT?
ARE YOU INSANE?

COME ON, WE'RE SO CLOSE TO FIGURING THIS OUT!
WE JUST HAVE TO FIND OUT WHAT'S IN THAT BOX!

MAYBE IT WILL LEAD US TO THE BODY!

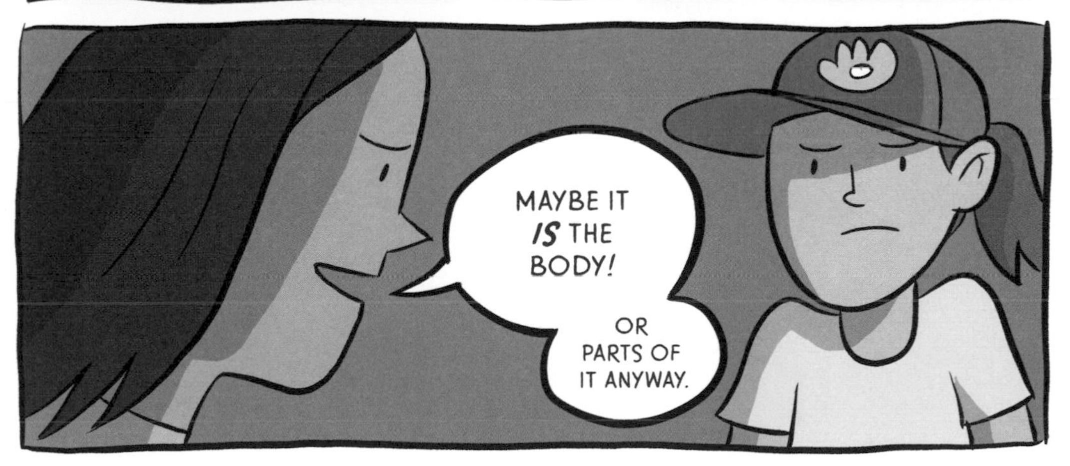
MAYBE IT IS THE BODY!
OR PARTS OF IT ANYWAY.

PAIGE! YOU'RE ACCUSING AN *INNOCENT MAN* OF MURDER!

WE DON'T *KNOW* HE'S INNOCENT. THAT'S THE WHOLE POINT!

FOR ALL WE KNOW, HE MIGHT HAVE KILLED HIS OWN WIFE TOO!

NO WAY! YOU'RE TAKING THIS TOO FAR.
ONLY ONE WAY TO FIND OUT.

NO! WE'RE NOT BREAKING INTO GENE'S HOUSE!
WHY NOT?

BECAUSE YOU'RE *OBSESSED!*

YOU ASKED ME TO HELP YOU SOLVE THIS MURDER!
TO WRITE A STORY! NOT TO FRAME SOMEONE!

THAT'S A CRIME, YOU KNOW. JUST LIKE MURDER, JUST LIKE STEALING, JUST LIKE TRESPASSING.

SO YOU *DO* THINK I'M A CRIMINAL, HUH?
YEAH, WELL...

IF THE SHOE FITS!

NONE OF THE RULES APPLY TO YOU, DO THEY?

AT LEAST I DON'T LIVE IN A *FANTASY* LAND!

OH PLEASE. WHAT ARE YOU EVEN TALKING ABOUT?

OH COME ON, GABBY. YOU'D RATHER WRITE A SAFE, *BORING STORY* WHERE YOU CAN CONTROL EVERYTHING AND EVERYONE.
YOU THINK YOU'RE SO MUCH *BETTER* THAN ME, BUT AT LEAST I TAKE RISKS.

YOU ARE BORING ON SO MANY LEVELS.
WELL YOU'RE JUST A...*JUVENILE DELINQUENT!*

WHATEVER, GO WRITE YOUR STUPID STORY, THEN.
HEY!

HEY!
HOW DO YOU THINK YOU'RE GETTING HOME, YOU JERK?
YOU CAN'T STEAL OUR KAYAK!
I'LL WALK!

HAVE FUN GETTING *TWO* KAYAKS HOME, GENIUS.

SLAM!

CLUNK
CLANK

THE NEXT MORNING...

I CAN'T BELIEVE WE HAVE TO SPEND OUR LAST DAY HOLED UP INSIDE.

HEY, MAYBE IF IT CLEARS UP BY THIS AFTERNOON WE CAN GET ONE LAST PONTOON RIDE IN.
YAY!
RING, RING

OH, I HAVE TO TAKE THIS.
RING

GREG, HEY. PLEASE TELL ME YOU'VE HEARD FROM CORPORATE...

THERE HE GOES AGAIN.
FOR ALL HIS TIME ON THE PHONE YOU'D THINK HE'D HAVE TOLD US WHERE WE'RE MOVING BY NOW.

GABBY, COME ON. YOU KNOW DAD'S GONE OUT OF HIS WAY TO MAKE THIS WEEK FUN FOR US.

OH YEAH, IT'S BEEN *REAL* FUN.
GEEZ, GABBY.

MAYBE IF YOU EVER QUIT READING FOR ONCE, YOU'D ACTUALLY *HAVE* SOME FUN.

I'M NOT READING, I'M WRITING.

BIG DIFFERENCE.
YOU'RE STILL CHOOSING YOUR FAKE WORLD OVER THE REAL WORLD.

JUST LIKE YOU ALWAYS DO.
I DON'T DO THAT!

NO OFFENSE, GABBY, BUT YOU KIND OF DO.
OH, LIKE *GLAM!* MAGAZINE IS THE REAL WORLD.

AND I ACTUALLY THOUGHT AFTER THE OTHER NIGHT WITH PAIGE AND BRYAN THAT YOU WERE MAYBE GONNA BE KIND OF FUN THIS WEEK!

I GUESS I WAS WRONG.

WAIT, WHAT HAPPENED WITH PAIGE AND BRYAN?

NOTHING!
COME ON, I'M BORED! CAN'T WE JUST *DO* SOMETHING?
HOP

GLAM!

WAIT, WHERE ARE YOU GOING, MORGAN?

I'M GONNA START PACKING.

DON'T LEAVE ME WITH THE BOOKWORM!
GABBY, WILL YOU HAVE MERCY ON SIMON AND PUT YOUR NOTEBOOK DOWN FOR A WHILE?

BELIEVE IT OR NOT, REAL LIFE CAN BE JUST AS EXCITING AS FICTION IF YOU JUST GIVE IT A SHOT!

KNOCK
KNOCK
KNOCK

I'LL GET IT.
WHOA, YOU GOT UP OFF THE COUCH, IT'S A MIRACLE!

HEY, GENE!
HI, KIDS!

I'M HEADING INTO TOWN AND WONDERED IF YOU FOLKS NEED ANYTHING?
SAVE YOU A TRIP OUT IN THIS RAIN!

UM, I DON'T THINK SO.
YEAH, WE'RE GOING HOME TOMORROW.

OH, SO SOON?
THIS WEEK REALLY FLEW BY!

WELL, IF YOU THINK OF ANYTHING, HAVE THEM PAGE ME AT PAUL BUNYAN'S.

BINGO DOESN'T START FOR ANOTHER HALF HOUR, SO I'VE GOT SOME TIME TO KILL!

SEE YA, GENE! GOOD LUCK AT BINGO!

SIMON, DID YOU HEAR THAT?

YEAH, "PAGE HIM"? WHAT DOES THAT EVEN MEAN? IS HE A BOOK?

NO, HE SAID HE HAS SOME "TIME TO KILL"?

TIME... TO ***KILL?***
UH, YEAH...PEOPLE SAY THAT ALL THE TIME.

YEAH...
BUT SOMETHING ABOUT THE WAY HE SAID IT...

SCREW IT. YOU STILL WANT TO DO SOMETHING?

WHAT'S GOING ON?
OKAY, YOU'RE GONNA THINK I'M CRAZY.

PAIGE AND I FOUND SOMETHING AT THE GOLDSWORTH HOUSE.
A BODY??

NO, BUT, LIKE, EVIDENCE.

EVIDENCE THAT DOESN'T LOOK GOOD FOR GENE.
GENE?

THE SAME GENE WHO JUST LEFT FOR BINGO?
YOU'RE TELLING ME HE WAS INVOLVED?

I'M TELLING YOU, HE...
HE MIGHT HAVE BEEN THE MURDERER.

HA-HA! GENE?

BUT PAIGE AND I SAW HIM OVER THERE YESTERDAY.
HE CAME INSIDE WITH HIS AX AND CHOPPED SOMETHING UP!

I KNOW, IT SOUNDS CRAZY.

AND THEN HE LEFT CARRYING A BOX!

WHAT WAS IN IT?

I DON'T KNOW. THAT'S WHAT WE'RE GONNA DO.
YOU AND ME.
UH...WHAT?

WE'RE GONNA SNEAK INTO GENE'S HOUSE AND FIND OUT.
RIGHT NOW?

YEAH! YOU KNOW HOW TO GET A WINDOW OPEN, RIGHT?
YEAH, BUT...

YOU WANTED ME TO GET OUT OF MY "FAKE WORLD," RIGHT?
YEAH, AND PLAY BOCCE BALL OR SOMETHING!

COME ON. WE HAVE TO FIND OUT WHAT'S IN THAT BOX.

I CAN'T BELIEVE WE'RE DOING THIS.
THINK OF IT AS ONE LAST ADVENTURE!
ZIP

HOW LONG WILL HE BE GONE?
I DUNNO, AN HOUR?

HENDERSON

LOCKED.
RATTLE

THERE'S NO KEY UNDER THE MAT.
NO HIDE-A-KEY EITHER.

THUNDER!

OKAY, TIME TO TRY A WINDOW.

IT'S SO DARK INSIDE...

DO YOU SEE ANYTHING?
NO, I DON'T THINK...
WAIT! LOOK ON THE TABLE!

THAT'S THE BOX!

WHAT IF IT HAS THEIR BONES IN IT?

UGH, I CAN'T EVEN THINK ABOUT THAT.

OKAY, SO HOW DO WE GET IN?
THIS WINDOW DOESN'T BUDGE.

MAYBE HE LEFT A DIFFERENT ONE UNLOCKED?
LET'S CIRCLE AROUND AND CHECK.

NO LUCK.
ME EITHER.

IT WAS SO EASY AT THE GOLDSWORTH HOUSE.

YEAH, BUT SOMEONE ACTUALLY LIVES HERE.

CAN YOU USE YOUR SCREWDRIVER TO TAKE ONE OF THE WINDOWS OFF?
NO WAY. THESE ARE NICE WINDOWS, NOT JANKY OLD GARAGE ONES.

UGH! WE *HAVE* TO GET IN THERE! SHOULD WE SMASH THE GLASS?

WE COULD SAY WE WERE PLAYING BASEBALL.
IN THE RAIN?
I DUNNO, WE HAVE TO DO *SOMETHING!*

OH, I KNOW!

WHEN BRYAN AND I WERE LOOKING AT THE GOLDSWORTH HOUSE, HE SAID YOU CAN SOMETIMES JUMP A SLIDING DOOR OFF ITS TRACK AND GET IN THAT WAY.

THOSE GUYS REALLY KNOW HOW TO BREAK INTO PLACES.
AND NOW WE DO TOO!

I THINK I CAN USE MY SCREWDRIVER TO PRY THE DOOR UP.
THEN YOU CAN PUSH THE DOOR IN.

OKAY, GREAT. BUT BE *CAREFUL!*

GIVE ME SOME ROOM.

creak
wiggle

IS IT WORKING?
I THINK I ALMOST GOT IT.

CRUUUUUNCH

CRUUUNNNNCH
WHAT'S THAT SOUND?
THUNDER?
NO, IT SOUNDS LIKE GRAVEL.

SOMEONE'S DRIVING UP!
OH CRAP.

COME ON, LET'S GO.
BUT THE BOX IS RIGHT THERE!

ARE YOU CRAZY? THAT IS PROBABLY GENE RIGHT NOW!
I DON'T SEE A CAR.

IT PROBABLY WAS THUNDER.

COME ON, WE CAN STILL DO THIS.
I'M OUTTA HERE!

!
WELL, *THIS* IS AN UNUSUAL RAINY DAY ACTIVITY.

SHERIFF RIVERA! I... I...

I GOT A CALL THERE WAS SOME SUSPICIOUS ACTIVITY AT THIS ADDRESS.
I'M GUESSING THAT WAS IN REGARDS TO YOU?
VRRRR

I CAN EXPLAIN.

SLAM

AFTERNOON, GENE.
HOWDY, SHERIFF.

IMAGINE MY SURPRISE WHEN I ARRIVED AT THE BINGO HALL TO A MESSAGE I SHOULD TURN AROUND AND HEAD BACK HOME.

I WAS FEELING LUCKY TODAY TOO.

SORRY, GENE.

GABBY WAS JUST ABOUT TO EXPLAIN HERSELF.

I WAS...JUST TRYING TO GET OUT OF THE RAIN?

AND YOU COULDN'T GO THE EXTRA TEN YARDS TO YOUR COTTAGE BECAUSE...
BECAUSE...

I'VE ALWAYS TOLD THE WOODS FAMILY THAT MY HOME WAS THEIR HOME.

I'M SURE IN THE THICK OF THE STORM GABBY WAS JUST THINKING OF THAT.

...WITH A SCREWDRIVER?

I SHOULD PROBABLY GET ONE OF THOSE HIDE-A-KEY ROCKS.

WELL IF YOU'RE NOT INTERESTED IN PURSUING THIS MATTER ANY FURTHER...
OF COURSE NOT.

THANK YOU FOR KEEPING AN EYE OUT THOUGH, SHERIFF.
MOST EXCITEMENT I'VE HAD ON THE LAKE ALL WEEK.

HEY, LOOKS LIKE THE RAIN'S CLEARED UP.
I'M SORRY YOU HAD TO MISS BINGO.

OH, I JUST GO FOR THE CONVERSATION.
MAYBE YOU AND I CAN HAVE A CHAT INSTEAD?

OKAY.
GREAT! I'LL GO GET US SOME LEMONADE AND A TOWEL TO DRY OFF THESE CHAIRS!

SO, WHAT HAVE YOU BEEN UP TO ON THIS DRIZZLY DAY?

MOSTLY I'VE BEEN WORKING ON MY STORY. TRYING TO ANYWAY.

THAT'S RIGHT, YOU AND PAIGE WERE WRITING ABOUT WALTER GOLDSWORTH, WEREN'T YOU?
YEAH.

IT KIND OF FELL APART THOUGH.
PAIGE AND I HAD SOME... CREATIVE DIFFERENCES.
AH YES. TEAMWORK IS A CHALLENGE! TWO PEOPLE CAN HAVE VERY DIFFERENT IDEAS.

YEAH, BUT IT'S NOT JUST THAT.
SHUFFF

WHAT IS IT?
WELL...

YOU KNEW HIM, DIDN'T YOU? GOLDSWORTH.
AH, I WAS WONDERING IF YOU MIGHT ASK ME ABOUT THAT.

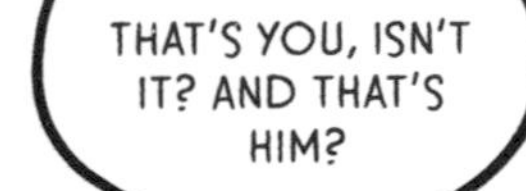

THAT'S YOU, ISN'T IT? AND THAT'S HIM?
YOU'RE RIGHT ABOUT THAT. MY, I WAS A BIT YOUNGER HERE, WASN'T I?

WAS THAT HIS WIFE?
YES, THAT WAS ANGELA MILLBROOK.

SHE WAS A FASHION MODEL FROM CHICAGO. VERY GLAMOROUS.

OH, DID HE LOVE HER.
DID...
DID YOU LOVE HER TOO?

ME?!

YEAH, UM, PAIGE HAS THIS THEORY THAT YOU AND ANGELA WERE HAVING AN AFFAIR.
AN *AFFAIR*, HUH?

YEAH, I MEAN, THIS IS SO *STUPID*, BUT...

SHE THINKS YOU AND ANGELA WERE HAVING AN AFFAIR AND WHEN WALTER FOUND OUT YOU KILLED HIM.
AND WHEN ANGELA SAW WHAT YOU DID...
YOU KILLED HER TOO.

SO I'M AN ADULTERER **AND** A MURDERER?

I KNOW, IT'S SO STUPID!
I WOULDN'T SAY IT'S STUPID... IT'S AN UNEXPECTED TWIST.

IT'S STILL JUST A MADE-UP STORY, RIGHT?

UM, WELL...

PAIGE IS KIND OF CONVINCED IT'S REAL NOW.

AH, I SEE! AND *YOU*?
...I DON'T KNOW WHAT TO THINK.

STRETCH
WELL...

I KNOW I DON'T HAVE TO TELL YOU HOW MUCH I LOVED MY WIFE.

I KNOW.

AND I HOPE IT GOES WITHOUT SAYING THAT I WOULD *NEVER* MURDER SOMEONE!
HA-HA...
IT SOUNDS SO FUNNY TO EVEN HEAR YOU SAY IT.

SO...WHAT *REALLY* DID HAPPEN AT THAT PLACE?
LOOK HERE.

THIS GAL RIGHT HERE, THAT WAS MS. EMILY BLOOM.

THAT'S THE WOMAN I WAS IN LOVE WITH.
AND NOT LONG AFTER THIS PICTURE WAS TAKEN, I MARRIED HER.

OH, THAT'S EMMY? SHE LOOKS SO YOUNG!
WE ALL WERE!

YOU NEVER HAD A THING WITH ANGELA?
HA-HA, NO. OH, SHE WAS A BEAUTIFUL WOMAN, SURE, BUT SHE DIDN'T HOLD A CANDLE TO MY EMMY.

AND IF MEMORY SERVES ME, WALT AND ANGELA WERE PRETTY CRAZY ABOUT EACH OTHER TOO.

SO WHAT HAPPENED? WHY'D THEY DISAPPEAR?

LET'S SEE. WHEN I FIRST MET WALTER HE HAD JUST FINISHED BUILDING HIS HOUSE.

HE WAS A THOUGHTFUL, TALENTED, AND INTELLIGENT MAN BUT SHY.
RKET

HE AND HIS WIFE DIDN'T KNOW ANYONE ON THE LAKE, SO EMMY AND I TOOK IT UPON OURSELVES TO BEFRIEND THEM. EMMY LIVED DOWN THE ROAD, AND SHE AND I WERE DATING AT THE TIME.
Jim's TAVERN FRIDAY FISH FRY 6 PM

FOR COMING FROM SUCH DIFFERENT BACKGROUNDS, THE FOUR OF US QUICKLY BECAME VERY DEAR FRIENDS. FOR THE NEXT COUPLE YEARS, WE WERE INSEPARABLE. BUT WE WANTED THE REST OF THE TOWN TO KNOW THIS COUPLE WE'D COME TO LOVE.

WE INTRODUCED THEM TO YOUR GRANDPARENTS AND OTHER FOLKS AROUND THE LAKE, AND SOON THEY HAD FOUND THEIR PLACE.

WE HAD NO IDEA, BUT ALL THIS TIME ANGELA WAS VERY SICK.

IT'S THE REASON THEY LEFT CHICAGO, TO GET HER SOMEWHERE PEACEFUL TO RECOVER.

WHEN THEY LEARNED SHE WASN'T GETTING BETTER, THEY FINALLY BROKE THE NEWS TO EMMY AND ME.

WE THREW THEM A PARTY AND INVITED ALL OF THEIR NEW FRIENDS FROM AROUND THE LAKE AND OLD FRIENDS BACK IN CHICAGO. IN A WAY IT WAS A GOODBYE PARTY, BUT MORE FOR HER THAN THEM, AS THEY DIDN'T TELL ANYONE BUT US THAT SHE WAS DYING.

THE NEXT DAY, SHE TOOK A TURN FOR THE WORSE AND THEY LEFT FOR CHICAGO IN QUITE A HURRY.
KOFF
KOF
KOFF

AS THEY LEFT SHE SAID, AND I'LL NEVER FORGET THIS:
THIS HOUSE IS A WORK OF ART. I'D HATE TO TARNISH IT BY DYING IN IT.

THEY WERE ONLY BACK IN CHICAGO FOR A FEW DAYS BEFORE SHE PASSED AWAY.
ANGELA GOLDSWORTH

WALTER WAS HEARTBROKEN.
HE NEVER WENT BACK TO THE HOUSE AND NEVER DESIGNED OR BUILT ANOTHER ONE.

WHAT HAPPENED TO HIM?

LIFE WENT ON, BUT HE DIDN'T DO MUCH LIVING.

HE KEPT A LOW PROFILE. BEGAN TO LOSE HIMSELF IN BOOKS. THERE WAS AN AIR OF MYSTERY AROUND HIM, ESPECIALLY SINCE HE HAD SHOWN SO MUCH PROMISE AS AN ARCHITECT, BUT EVENTUALLY PEOPLE MOVED ON AND MORE OR LESS FORGOT ABOUT HIM.

WE STAYED IN TOUCH, BUT HE WASN'T THE SAME. HE DIED YOUNG, OF A HEART ATTACK.

SHORTLY AFTER THAT WE RECEIVED A LETTER WE WOULD NEVER FORGET.

IT WAS REGARDING WALTER'S WILL. HE HAD LEFT THE HOUSE TO EMMY AND ME.

THAT HOUSE BELONGS TO YOU?
IT DOES.

WHY DON'T YOU LIVE THERE?

WE COULD NEVER BRING OURSELVES TO MOVE INTO IT.
THE MEMORY OF LOSING BOTH ANGELA AND WALTER WAS TOO PAINFUL.

I STOP IN FROM TIME TO TIME TO DO SOME MAINTENANCE.
MAYBE ONE DAY I'LL OPEN IT UP TO PEOPLE.

ANYWAY, NOW YOU KNOW WHAT REALLY HAPPENED THERE.
OH.

NOT QUITE AS EXCITING AS A *DOUBLE MURDER*, IS IT?
NO. BUT I GUESS THAT'S GOOD.

I THINK YOU SHOULD FINISH YOUR STORY THOUGH. WITH THE TWIST.
I DON'T MIND IF YOU MAKE ME THE BAD GUY.

IN FACT, IT'S KIND OF AN *HONOR* TO BE IN A MYSTERY AT ALL.
REALLY?
YEAH!

NOW, I WONDER WHERE YOU FOUND THIS PICTURE.
...CAN I BLAME PAIGE FOR THAT?

TO BE HONEST, I'M NOT TOO CONCERNED ABOUT IT.

IT'S BRIGHTENED MY DAY TO SEE IT AND TO HAVE THIS CHAT WITH YOU.

NOW I ONLY WISH I COULD READ THAT MYSTERY.
SOUNDS LIKE PAIGE WAS A PRETTY GOOD WRITING PARTNER.
YEAH.

HEY, LOOKS LIKE YOUR DAD IS GETTING READY TO SET SAIL.

YOU'VE GOT A REAL GREAT FAMILY, GABBY.

GOOD PARENTS WHO CARE ABOUT YOU.

YOU KNOW THAT, RIGHT?
YEAH.
I DO.

HEY, DAD.

OH, HEY, GABBY!

YOU BEEN WORKING ON YOUR STORY?
YEAH, KIND OF.

EVERYTHING OKAY?
I GUESS...
PAT

HEY LOOK, I KNOW THIS HASN'T BEEN AN EASY WEEK FOR YOU.

MAYBE I SHOULDN'T HAVE SAID ANYTHING ABOUT THE JOB UNTIL I KNEW FOR SURE.

I GUESS I JUST WANTED TO GIVE YOU A CHANCE TO PREPARE, BUT I THINK I MADE THINGS HARDER.

WHAT I'M TRYING TO SAY IS, I'M SORRY.

YOU DON'T HAVE TO SAY SORRY!

I'M THE ONE WHO SHOULD SAY SORRY!

I'VE BEEN A JERK ALL WEEK.

WELL, LET'S CALL IT EVEN, THEN.

I LOVE YOU, GABBY.

NOW LET'S TAKE THIS BOAT OUT FOR A SPIN! WHAT DO YOU SAY?

I SAY LET'S DO IT!
Put put put
THUMP
THUMP

TIME TO *SINK* THIS BOAT!

YOU INVITED BRYAN'S FAMILY?

I THOUGHT IT WOULD BE NICE.
I'LL ACCEPT THAT APOLOGY NOW.

OH COME ON, IT WILL BE FUN.

HEY, GABBY... SORRY I BAILED ON YOU BEFORE.
YEAH, WHAT THE HECK? THAT'LL TEACH ME TO HAVE AN ADVENTURE WITH YOU!
WHAT HAPPENED?

GENE'S NOT MAD. I THINK HE EVEN COVERED FOR US.
AND THEN WE JUST TALKED.

DID YOU FIND OUT...
NOT WHAT'S IN THE BOX...

BUT HE'S DEFINITELY ***NOT*** A MURDERER!
PHEW!

SOUNDS LIKE SOMEBODY CAUGHT A *RED HERRING!*

HEY, BRYAN, WHERE'S PAIGE?
OH, SHE'S NOT COMING.

SHE'S PRETTY MUCH LOCKED HERSELF IN HER ROOM SINCE THE LAST TIME YOU GUYS HUNG OUT.

DID YOU GUYS HAVE A FIGHT OR SOMETHING?
I GUESS.

WELL, IT'S STARTING TO FEEL LIKE WE MIGHT NEVER SEE HER AGAIN, SO...THANK YOU!

WELCOME ABOARD! GLAD YOU COULD JOIN US!

OH, WE ARE SO EXCITED! THIS IS OUR FIRST TIME ON A PONTOON BOAT.

THIS THING SEAWORTHY?
HASN'T LET US DOWN YET.

HEY, DAD, CAN I STEER IT?
OOH, AND THEN ME?

YOU CAN BOTH GET A TURN WHEN WE ARE OUT IN OPEN WATER.

YEAH!
DON'T MAKE ME REGRET THIS!

PAUL, JANE, CAN I GET YOU ANYTHING TO DRINK?
I'LL TAKE A COLD ONE.
YES, SAME FOR ME.

SO WHAT'S YOUR LINE OF WORK, DARREN?

I'M IN THE PAPER BUSINESS.
ALTHOUGH I'M LUCKY TO HAVE A JOB AT ALL.

OUR COMPANY WAS JUST ACQUIRED BY A "BIG FISH," SO TO SPEAK.

THIS ECONOMY! I TELL YOU.

HOW ABOUT YOU FOLKS, WHAT DO YOU DO?

OH, WE'RE ATTORNEYS.

PLEASE DON'T THROW US OVERBOARD!

OH, I THOUGHT GABBY SAID YOU WERE ACCOUNTANTS.

ACCOUNTANTS? NO, NOT US.

NO, WE'RE DEFENSE ATTORNEYS.

MAYBE SHE MISUNDERSTOOD.

NO, I DIDN'T.

WHAT'S THAT, HONEY?

I DIDN'T MISUNDERSTAND. PAIGE TOLD ME YOU WERE ACCOUNTANTS.
I REMEMBER 'CUZ IT SOUNDED SO BORING.

WELL, LAST I CHECKED WE WERE DEFENSE ATTORNEYS...

AT LEAST THAT'S WHAT WE'VE BEEN GETTING PAID FOR!

DO YOU DO *ANYTHING* WITH ACCOUNTING?

NO, DEAR. JUST DEFENSE. SOMETIMES OUR PAIGE...WELL...
SHE CAN BEND THE TRUTH A LITTLE.

SHE *LIES.*
GABBY!

SOMETIMES SHE LIES.

I DON'T KNOW WHERE SHE GETS IT.
HA HA HA

Swerve!

SORRY!
I THOUGHT I SAW A LOG!

LATER...

I DON'T GET IT.

WHY WOULD SHE *LIE* ABOUT THAT?
WHO KNOWS.
LEGAL STUFF CAN BE PRETTY CONFUSING, MAYBE SHE JUST GOT MIXED UP.

OR MAYBE SHE'S JUST A LIAR.

WELL, WE LEAVE TOMORROW, SO YOU'LL BE RID OF HER SOON ENOUGH.

YEAH, I GUESS IT DOESN'T MATTER.

YOU GUYS FEEL LIKE ONE LAST BONFIRE TONIGHT?
DEFINITELY.
CAN I INVITE BRYAN?

YOU KNOW WHAT? I THINK BRYAN MIGHT BURN THE WHOLE PLACE DOWN, SO MAYBE NOT.

BESIDES...

I WANT TO TALK TO YOU GUYS ABOUT SOME STUFF.

KSSSS

SNAP
SNAP
sizzle

PASS ME THE MARSHMALLOWS, MORGAN!

YOU KIDS BE CAREFUL!
LET'S NOT END THE WEEK WITH A TRIP TO THE ER.

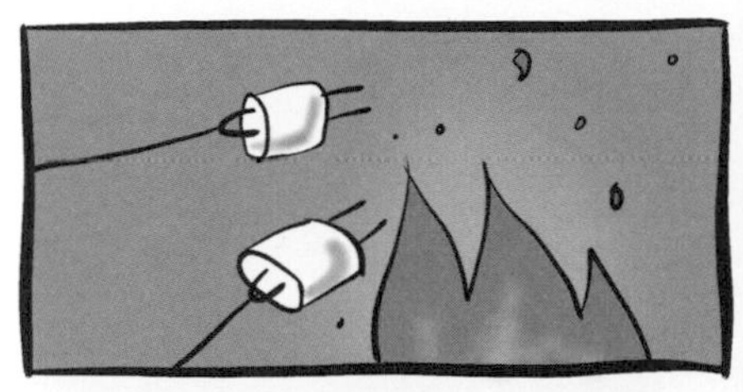

WELL, NOW THAT EVERYONE'S ON A SUGAR HIGH, IT MIGHT BE A GOOD TIME TO TELL YOU...

I FOUND OUT WHERE I'M BEING TRANSFERRED.

UH-OH.
IS IT ATLANTA?

NOPE, WE'LL BE STAYING IN THE MIDWEST. JUST ONE STATE OVER.

ST. PAUL, MINNESOTA!

MINNESOTA?
OKAY, THEY TALK FUNNY THERE TOO.
HA-HA.
ALL RIGHT, LET'S LOOK AT THE POSITIVES.

IT'S JUST FOUR HOURS FROM HOME.

MORGAN, WE'LL ACTUALLY BE EVEN CLOSER TO YOUR COLLEGE THAN BEFORE.

MAYBE EVEN A LITTLE *TOO* CLOSE?
OH GOODY.

WE'LL START LOOKING AT HOUSES SOON, BUT IT'S A VERY NICE CITY.

THAT'S *VIKINGS* TERRITORY.

I HEAR THERE ARE SOME PACKERS FANS THERE TOO.

THERE ARE GREAT SCHOOLS, PARKS, MUSEUMS...

IT'S EVEN COLDER THAN GREEN BAY.

TRUE. BUT THAT'S BETTER THAN SUMMERS IN "HOT-LANTA," RIGHT?

THE COMPANY WANTS ME THERE PRETTY SOON, SO THEY'RE GOING TO PUT US UP IN CORPORATE HOUSING WHILE WE GET SETTLED.
CORPA-WHAT?

IT'S LIKE A BIG FURNISHED APARTMENT.
BUT KIND OF MORE LIKE A HOTEL...

WE'LL HAVE A SWIMMING POOL.
NICE!

AND MAID SERVICE...
YEAH!

DON'T GET USED TO IT.

GABBY, AREN'T YOU GOING TO ASK ME ABOUT THE BEST PART?

WHAT'S THE BEST PART?

THE BEST PART IS... WE GET TO KEEP THE COTTAGE.
WE DO?

LOOKS LIKE ALL YOUR POUTING PAID OFF, GABBY!

WE'LL BE BACK HERE NEXT SUMMER, LORD WILLING, AND MANY SUMMERS TO COME.

OKAY, I GUESS I'LL HAVE *ONE* MORE S'MORE TO TOAST TO THAT!
HAPPY

LONG LIVE THE COTTAGE!

OOH! I KNOW JUST HOW TO CELEBRATE!

SNAP!

HEY!
HEY!

BRYAN!
NOW WHAT IS HE UP TO?

SHE HAD HER BABIES!
WHO DID?

SANDY!

THE BABIES ARE HERE!
WHO'S SANDY?

HOW DID THIS KID GET IN OUR GARAGE?

THIS SIDE UP

STOP! NO CLOSER!

SHE JUST HAD BABIES, GIVE HER SOME SPACE!

WERE YOU HERE WHEN SHE HAD THEM?
NO, I CAME IN THIS MORNING AND SAW THESE GUYS.
BRYAN AND I JUST CHECKED HER LAST NIGHT AND SHE WAS STILL BIG AS A BLIMP!
MEW!
THEIR LITTLE MEOWS ARE SO CUTE!

THEY LOOK LIKE LITTLE WET RATS.

YOU PROBABLY LOOKED LIKE A RAT WHEN YOU WERE BORN!

GEEZ, WHAT'S WITH THIS KID?

SHUFFF
WELL, WHAT HAVE WE HERE?

KITTENS!

DID YOU ALL KNOW WE HAD A SQUATTER IN OUR GARAGE?
WE KNEW.

WHAT SHOULD WE DO? WE GO HOME TODAY!
WE CAN'T JUST LEAVE THEM HERE!

THE MAMA KNOWS HOW TO TAKE CARE OF THEM.

AND MY FAMILY WILL BE AROUND FOR A WHILE STILL.

MAYBE BRYAN CAN KEEP AN EYE ON THEM.
I WILL!

I ALREADY NAMED THEM. THIS IS GRASSY, THAT'S ROCKY, MUDDY, AND THE LITTLE ONE IS TURTLE.

ALL RIGHT, BRYAN, YOU KEEP A GOOD WATCH! WE NEED TO GET BACK TO PACKING.
OUR VACATION IS OVER.

AT LEAST UNTIL NEXT SUMMER.

UM, I'LL BE RIGHT BACK, OKAY?

HEY, PAIGE.

YOU DIDN'T GO ON THE PONTOON RIDE LAST NIGHT.
I WAS SICK.

I KNOW YOU WERE JUST AVOIDING ME, BUT THAT'S FINE.

CHICAGO

YOUR MOM AND DAD AREN'T ACCOUNTANTS.
NOPE.

WHO BLEW MY COVER? BRYAN?

NO, YOUR MOM TOLD ME. THEY'RE *DEFENSE ATTORNEYS.*

YUP.
CHICAGO

I DON'T GET IT, WHY WOULD YOU *LIE* ABOUT THAT?

OH, I DUNNO, BECAUSE MY PARENTS DEFEND *CRIMINALS* FOR A LIVING?
CHICAGO

YOU DON'T THINK THERE'S ANYTHING UNCOOL ABOUT THAT?

WELL...EVERYONE HAS A RIGHT TO A DEFENSE. I MEAN, IT'S IN THE CONSTITUTION.
INNOCENT UNTIL PROVEN GUILTY, RIGHT?

SURE, IT SOUNDS ALL NOBLE AND PATRIOTIC WHEN YOU SAY IT LIKE THAT, BUT YOU DON'T GET IT.
CHICAGO

TRUST ME.
THERE'S NOTHING ADMIRABLE ABOUT WHAT MY PARENTS DO.

WHAT DO YOU MEAN?

GABBY, MY PARENTS ARE THE MARTINS.
THE *WHO*?
PAUL AND JANE MARTIN? *SERIOUSLY*?

OH COME ON. YOU'VE HEARD OF THE LUMENS TRIAL, RIGHT?
IT WAS *ALL OVER* THE NEWS THIS SUMMER.

OH YEAH, A LITTLE. I HEARD MY PARENTS TALKING ABOUT IT SOMETIMES.
THAT WAS SOME RICH GUY WHO WAS ACCUSED OF MURDERING A REPORTER, RIGHT?

YEAH. AND THAT RICH GUY HAD EXPENSIVE LAWYERS, AND THOSE *LAWYERS* ARE MY *PARENTS*.
WHOA, FOR REAL?

YEP. THE "MOST DISTINGUISHED LEGAL TEAM IN THE MIDWEST." TOTAL BULL CRAP.
WELL THEY DID WIN THEIR CASE, RIGHT?
YEAH, EXACTLY.
BUT DO YOU THINK LUMENS WAS ACTUALLY *INNOCENT*?

I DUNNO. WASN'T HE?

GEEZ, GABBY, YOU'RE *OBSESSED* WITH MURDER STORIES, I CAN'T BELIEVE YOU WEREN'T PAYING MORE ATTENTION!
OKAY, LET ME CATCH YOU UP...

HARRIS LUMENS IS A CON MAN WHO LIES, CHEATS, AND SWINDLES PEOPLE ON A REGULAR BASIS AND ALWAYS GETS AWAY WITH IT.
SOLD
LUMENS REALTY

THAT REPORTER GUY WAS JUST TRYING TO DO THE RIGHT THING, TO EXPOSE HIM FOR WHO HE WAS.

BUT HE GOT TOO CLOSE, SO LUMENS HAD HIM KILLED. HE PAID FOR HIS MURDER. THAT MAKES HIM A MURDERER.
15
17

HE'S GUILTY. EVERYBODY KNOWS HE'S GUILTY. THEY HAVE A RIDICULOUS AMOUNT OF EVIDENCE, INCLUDING A FRICKIN' TAPED CONFESSION.

BUT HE'S GOT A LOT OF MONEY. AND BECAUSE MY PARENTS ARE SUCH A "DISTINGUISHED LEGAL TEAM" HE GOT OFF ON A TECHNICALITY.

BUT DO YOU THINK MY PARENTS *CARE* IF HE WAS GUILTY OR NOT?

OF COURSE THEY DON'T!
THEY JUST GO WHERE THE MONEY IS. THEY ALWAYS HAVE.

THEY GOT A MASSIVE PAYCHECK FOR THIS CASE, AND THEY'RE, LIKE, CELEBRITIES NOW.

EXCEPT THEY'RE THE KIND OF CELEBRITIES THAT EVERYONE *HATES.*

SPLISH!

WE GOT *DEATH THREATS* AFTER THE TRIAL.

WOW! IS THAT WHY YOU GUYS CAME UP HERE?
YEAH.

TO GET AWAY FROM THE BAD PRESS AND THE HARASSMENT, AND MY PARENTS' GUILTY CONSCIENCES I'M SURE.
SHRUG

FUN VACATION, HUH?

WELL, I KNOW IT SEEMS WRONG, BUT EVERYONE HAS A RIGHT TO A LAWYER, RIGHT?

THAT'S HOW OUR LEGAL SYSTEM WORKS.
YEAH, WHATEVER.

THIS REPORTER WHO WAS KILLED, HE HAD A WIFE AND A LITTLE BOY. AND HIS FAMILY WILL NEVER HAVE JUSTICE.

THANKS TO MY PARENTS.

YOU KNOW, FOR A LONG TIME I TRIED TO GIVE MY PARENTS HELL BY BEING A "BAD KID."
SMOKING, SWEARING, STEALING, WHATEVER. BUT I'VE HAD AN EPIPHANY.

I'M GONNA BE A LAWYER TOO ONE DAY.
DISTRICT ATTORNEY OR SOMETHING.

I COULD ACTUALLY SEE THAT!

PSH, DON'T SAY "ACTUALLY" LIKE IT'S A BIG SURPRISE.
I'D MAKE AN *AWESOME* LAWYER!

AND I'D MAKE SURE PEOPLE LIKE HARRIS LUMENS DON'T WALK.

COME ON, GET UP.
THANKS.
SO, IS THAT WHY YOU WANTED TO SOLVE THE GOLDSWORTH MYSTERY?

I STILL THINK GENE IS GUILTY!

BUT...MAYBE I GOT A LITTLE CARRIED AWAY.

I GUESS WE'LL NEVER KNOW WHAT REALLY HAPPENED.

ACTUALLY, I ASKED GENE ABOUT IT.
CHICAGO BEARS

YOU DID NOT!

YEAH, HE TOLD ME WHAT HAPPENED.

WELL COUGH IT UP! WHAT *WAS* IT?

HATE TO DISAPPOINT YOU, BUT THERE WERE NO MURDERS, NO AFFAIRS. JUST SOME SAD REAL-LIFE HEALTH STUFF.
AND GET THIS, THAT HOUSE ACTUALLY BELONGS TO GENE.

WHAT? HOW? IS HE *REALLY GOLDSWORTH*? DID HE STEAL GOLDSWORTH'S IDENTITY?

SHRUG
CHICAGO

SERIOUSLY? THAT'S ALL YOU'RE GONNA GIVE ME? NO JUICY DETAILS?

IF YOU CAN WITHHOLD INFORMATION, I CAN TOO.
CHICAGO

OH, I'LL GET IT OUT OF YOU.

ANYWAY. SORRY I LIED TO YOU ABOUT MY PARENTS.
AND THAT I KIND OF TOOK OVER YOUR STORY.
IT'S OKAY.

I HAD A LOT OF FUN WRITING IT WITH YOU.

MAYBE WE COULD KEEP WORKING ON IT TOGETHER?
REALLY?
UNZZZIP
AREN'T YOU GUYS LEAVING TODAY?

YEAH BUT WE COULD SEND IT TO EACH OTHER?
LIKE PEN PALS.

GIVE ME YOUR ADDRESS?
CHICAGO

PEN PALS, HUH?
I THOUGHT I WAS JUST A COMMON CRIMINAL IN YOUR BOOK.

I SHOULDN'T HAVE SAID THAT.
YOU...

YES?
...YOU HELPED ME GET OUT OF MY HEAD A LITTLE BIT. AND THE WORLD DIDN'T END OR ANYTHING.
SO THANKS.

WOW, THAT'S ALMOST AN APOLOGY?
ALMOST.

YOU'RE NOT *COMPLETELY* WRONG ABOUT ME THOUGH.

?
CHICAGO

STAR TREK
Mission to Horatius

Flip
STAR TREK
PROPERTY of Walter Goldsworth

YOU STOLE THIS? FROM GOLDSWORTH'S BOOKCASE?
I CAN'T HELP IT, IT'S A BAD HABIT!

IT'S THE *MISSION TO HORATIUS,* GABBY. THAT'S THE FIRST ORIGINAL *STAR TREK* NOVEL EVER PUBLISHED!
JUST SITTING ON AN ABANDONED BOOKSHELF, ***THAT'S*** THE CRIME.

SO YOU ***ARE*** A NERD.
DON'T TELL MY BROTHER.

MAYBE YOU CAN GIVE IT BACK TO GENE?

YOU CAN GIVE IT BACK TO GENE YOURSELF.
KNOWING HIM, HE'LL MOST LIKELY TELL YOU TO KEEP IT.

WELL, SEE YA NEXT SUMMER, I GUESS. GOOD LUCK WITH YOUR *LEGAL CAREER!*
YEAH, YEAH.
HAVE A NICE LIFE, *NANCY DREW.*

OKAY, LIFT ON THREE...
ONE, TWO, THREE!

OKAY, CAREFUL NOW, JUST OVER THE RACK...
GOT THE ROPES, SIMON?
GOT 'EM!
BE CAREFUL!

LOOK WHO MANAGED TO AVOID THE HEAVY LIFTING.
SORRY!

FOR THAT, YOU HAVE TO SIT IN THE WAY BACK SEAT!
GOOD, I **LIKE** THE WAY BACK.

WE SURE HAD A NICE WEEK, DIDN'T WE?
MY LITTLE WRITER.
THANKS FOR YOUR HELP, GENE!
NO PROBLEM!

OH, GABBY, I HAVE SOMETHING FOR YOU!

I'VE BEEN THINKING ABOUT YOUR MYSTERY A LOT AND I WANTED TO HELP OUT.

OF COURSE THERE'S NOTHING QUITE LIKE AN IMAGINATION, BUT...

THIS MIGHT HELP YOU FILL IN SOME OF THE HOLES.

OH... WHAT'S IN IT?

JUST SOME KEEPSAKES, REALLY.
A LOT OF MEMORIES.

TAVERN
WOOD CHOP CHAMPION
BINGO

I'VE BEEN HANGING ON TO THEM FOR YEARS, BUT I THINK YOU AND PAIGE COULD PUT THEM TO CREATIVE USE.

WOW. THANKS, GENE!

DON'T FORGET, I WANT A COPY OF THAT STORY WHEN IT'S DONE!

ALL RIGHT, FAM!
ALL ABOARD WHO'S COMING ABOARD!
BYE, GENE!

CLICK
UH-OH, SHE'S GOT THAT LOOK IN HER EYE.

NO ONE BOTHER GABBY FOR THE NEXT THREE HOURS...
SHE'S OFF TO FANTASY LAND!

WHAT'S IN THE BOX?
OH, JUST SOME STORY STUFF.

IT CAN WAIT THOUGH.
SHUT

YOU GOT THAT DECK OF CARDS, SIMON?

IT'S TIME FOR AN *EPIC* GAME OF CHEAT!

ACKNOWLEDGMENTS

Thank you so much to the following people: Everyone at Scholastic/Graphix, especially David Saylor, Phil Falco, Cassandra Pelham Fulton; my fantastic editor Adam Rau; Aron Nels Steinke for pointing me in a great direction; Jonathan Hill for being my comics buddy from the beginning and giving the best advice; Simone Lia for your encouragement and solidarity; Jamie Letourneau for the eleventh-hour color cleanup; earliest readers Graham Murtaugh, Mollye Glennen, and Holly Trasti; my mom and dad, sister Meagan, and brother Shawn for a lifetime of support and constant inspiration; my kids, Harvey and Helen, who were so patient as I worked on this book; and my incredible husband, Zech, who has championed me and this book in every way imaginable. To everyone who has read my stories and cheered me on along the way — from the bottom of my heart, thank you!

BREENA BARD writes and illustrates comics, drawing inspiration from her childhood in Wisconsin and the stacks of graphic novels on her bedside table. She lives in Portland, Oregon, with her husband, two kids, and cranky but lovable cat.